The Silver Bird

A TALE FOR THOSE WHO DREAM

Joyce Petschek

ILLUSTRATIONS BY STEPHEN SNELL

CELESTIAL ARTS
MILLBRAE, CALIFORNIA

Celestial Arts
231 Adrian Rd.
Millbrae, CA 94030

First Printing, April 1981
First Hardcover Edition, April 1982

Cover painting by Stephen Snell
Manufactured in the United States of America

Library of Congress Cataloging in Publication Data

Petschek, Joyce
   The silver bird

   1. Petschek, Joyce   2. Occult sciences—
Biography.   I. Title.
BF1408.2.P47A37   133.9′3   80-28074
ISBN 0-89087-345-3 (hc)
ISBN 0-89087-359-3 (ppb)

1 2 3 4 5 6 7   88 87 86 85 84 83 82

To Robbie, Nicky and Carla
each one a dream who became a reality

Contents

Introduction

THIS IS A REAL STORY about real people. It became a tale-to-be-told when a dream said it would be. In our Tuscany house, where sleepy nights and sunshine days unroll into one continuous wave, was where it began. The Fall of 1976 offered two prophetic dreams. Yet nothing happened until four months later. Like a flowing river, the course was determined long before I discovered it was going anywhere.

The first dream was familiar in theme. Egyptian pyramids, with secret chambers and dark passageways, flashed through my vision. A faraway voice spoke asking if I had further questions about ancient Egypt. "No, I did not," I heard myself answer. Then a Silver Bird approached. Made of glistening silver, finely etched and polished, I could rest it in the palm of my hand. After that I awoke, remembering little else.

The second dream occurred the next night. Now appeared a Tibetan-looking man seated behind a long table, one strewn with many papers. Engrossed in reading the documents before him, he paid little attention to me. Then, slowly raising his eyes, he looked piercingly through me and inquired if I remembered the Silver Bird. "Yes," was my reply. "Good," he answered, "I was the one who gave it to you." He pointed to the Bird now perched on the table. After shuffling the papers again, he said, "You have passed your tests. Your work is about to begin." And that was all.

Stunned, I wondered what this could mean.

At that time I was involved in research concerned with tele-pathic communication, that which happens in the deep states of relaxation. As my 'dream-screen' had been movie-like since childhood, this exploration expanded my interests. I started writing a factual account about the group projects. But after com-pleting the first chapter, all copies disappeared, nowhere to be found. Again the dream-voice returned. Now it said, "You are to write a fantasy." "A fantasy?" I replied, decidedly uncomfortable with the idea. Soon I realized this meant not just a fantastic story but an experience in itself: the journey one takes when joining the 'outer and inner' worlds. I closed my eyes and was shown this book . . . .

Then I understood: 'the work' was about to begin!

Every morning for months thereafter I would awaken, appre-hensive and dizzy, my body and mind not quieting until I sat at the typewriter and witnessed a story form before my eyes. When doubt overcame me, a chapter would be skipped, to be written later when I was more trusting. The story meshed my inward and outward life, often playing tricks with my mind. Soon my dreams seemed like reality, while the experiences of reality became the dream.

The drawings happened the same way.

Years before they were created, I was guiding someone in the dream-state. Suddenly her vision was interrupted by a voice saying, "Somebody is going to be very artistic, draw very well. They have psychic faculty and, if you describe something they will know what you mean and be able to draw it for you, exactly

as you see it, although they actually can't see it themselves."
Then she continued 'mind-traveling' through tunnels beneath
the earth as if nothing had been said. That was also in 1976. Two
years later, when seeking an artist to illustrate the book, I saw
Stephen Snell's drawing at another artist's house. At my request
he was given a manuscript to read. A few days later he tele-
phoned saying, "You write in pictures. I see all your pictures and,
if you don't let me illustrate your book, I shall do so anyway.
Then you will regret not having chosen me."

How could I resist?

And so began our cooperative venture. Only later did I learn
that Stephen was a factory worker, having completed only one
drawing and one painting to date! Yet his desire to be an artist
was an old one. The closest to its happening had been a teaching
visit to Ernst Fuchs in Vienna. His dream became real with our
creating together. I would visualize the picture in my mind.
Stephen would draw what he 'saw'. Later he added details, as
'little people' hidden in the grass, saying I had forgotten them.
Each time he claimed the picture was impossible to draw. Each
time he returned with one more beautiful than the next.

What more can I say?

Dreams have always been my real life. They have been how I
experience existence. Many people I believe have lived the same
way. Now I wish to share my dreams with you, wondering if you
have lived like this as well.

Joyce Petschek
London, 1981

xi

The Silver Bird

Once upon a time, I, Chuang Tzŭ, dreamt I was a butterfly, fluttering hither and thither, to all intents and purposes a butterfly, and was unconscious of my individuality as a man. Suddenly, I awaked, and there I lay, myself again. Now I do not know whether I was then a man dreaming I was a butterfly, or whether I am now a butterfly, dreaming I am a man.

CHUANG TZŬ
Taoist Philosopher and Chinese Mystic
c. 330 B.C.

I

The Beginning

*I*T HAD BEEN RAINING all day. The wind was howling, the water so thick against the windowpane, I couldn't see the trees outside. I tried to clear the steam away, but nothing helped. Usually rainy days were comforting. I would stay in my bedroom, play quiet games, read and just dream.

But this day was terror.

Mother had been scolding me since morning. And the strong smell of sulphur, clinging to my body in fear, wouldn't leave. Although no one spoke a word, there was trouble between my parents. It inevitably happened on nurse's day off.

And today was no different.

Except now rain, hammering like beating drums, was pouring against the house. For the hundredth time, Mother repeated that I was born in a thunderstorm, the worst ever. Like a lightning bolt, unwanted and threatening, was how I always felt.

For me rain was warm and comforting. For Mother it was something she couldn't control. She became irrational, saying things she never did on other days. In turn, I became a frightened rabbit, scurrying to get away from her.

Nothing I said that day was right, nothing pleased her. Perhaps it was the nightdress I hadn't put in the hamper, the oatmeal that stuck in my throat, the green crayon mark on my white pinafore. I didn't know where to go, where to hide. By afternoon I was in tears, head hidden under my pillow, silently crying, lest anyone should hear.

I sobbed for what seemed hours.

Then a familiar voice called, "You are chosen! You are chosen!"

Bitter and angry, I replied, "Chosen? Chosen for WHAT?"

I stared into the mirror. My face was red and puffy, with deep circles under my eyes. Sad and forlorn, a lost little girl, no one to talk to, no one to play with, no one to explain what was happening. My younger sister was always whimpering, my elder brother tormented me with snakes. All nurse cared about were taffeta ribbons in my hair. Children were puppets to be seen not heard, either 'good' or 'bad'.

But to a small one, who wasn't certain what *was* right or wrong, what did it matter?

Like a marionette on a string, I dangled between the adults. My one wish was to be far from the arguments, the endless moralizing. Why couldn't they see I was a Queen ruling *my* kingdom with love and fairness? That I could tell their words before they spoke them? I saw a red halo around their heads when they were angry, a green halo when they cared. The circus colors changed as their moods shifted. No matter how calm they looked outside, the sparks that flew were electric, fireworks in the air.

The adults knew nothing of my thoughts.

Instead, they made a little servant of me, carrying white folded notes from Mother to Father on the days they weren't speaking to each other. Father would come in the evening. The messenger of peace. He would summarize my naughtiness, how I had angered Mother that day, the cause of all their trouble. I would stare empty-minded, pretend to listen but fade away—sometimes so blank I never heard a word he said. The words came from his head, not his heart. I felt his whirlpool of confusion, his embarrassment, his wish that we should talk of other things.

An awkwardness grew in those times.

Caught between these mountains, I only sought escape.

But how? And to where?

The dreams had always been with me.

I dreamed forever; dreamed of forgotten lands, of magical worlds, of faraway planets and singing stars, of another mother, even a father.

I found a "pretend" cottage, one hidden deep between the trees. Each afternoon, and in times of trouble, I ventured to this dream haven, disguised in a simple blue gown. My long hair would be free and flowing, with pink flowers tucked here and there.

The cottage door was so low I had to stoop to enter. But once inside, I sat upon a tiny stool and sipped tomato juice that was waiting on the checkered tablecloth. The small dark room was always silent. No voices disturbed my thoughts, no one criticized my manners.

Often fairies came to play, singing alluring songs only I could hear. I would find them nestled in the rose garden, lightly touching each crimson and coral petal. Their bodies were soft clouds of color, their misty wings of green and lavender and mauve. Less than a foot tall, they floated silently in and out of buds and bushes. And when they rested on my arm, I could look through each filmy garment and see their lithesome bodies glide in waves of light.

I had to watch them sideways, out of the corner of my eye.

If I stared directly at them, they would vanish.

Sometimes bands of fairies came to play, with golden stars glistening in their hair. They danced to my nonsense rhymes, laughing the moments away. They didn't care about the arithmetic I hadn't understood, the broken porcelain in the drawing room, the milk I spilled at breakfast. They loved the pictures I painted in the air. And how the leaves shook from my laughter.

What happened at the cottage was kept to myself.

That way nothing could be spoiled.

Yet none of the pieces fitted together.

The family quarrel was like a frustrated dragon caught in a smoldering house surrounded by an idyllic landscape.

Everything inside was turbulent. Everything outside was tranquil.

The woods were thick and abundant, the pink cherry trees blossomed every springtime. There were blue delphiniums and yellow and purple hollyhocks in the garden, a looking-glass lake, and peacocks strutting about.

The house itself had a quiet, yet elusive, personality. Its timbered beams came from the nearby forest, its huge fireplaces were carved of native stone. Sunlight fell through its leaded windows casting flickering patterns on the oak floors. Edward, a legend unto himself, polished the oak to mirror brightness, singing pious hymns as he worked. He spoke to me of God before I was old enough to understand what he was saying.

The house was a treasure chest, an Aladdin's cave, filled with silver heirlooms and faded, brown photographs. Abundance lay everywhere, but it was its dark corners I sought. How often I climbed the well-worn steps to the musty attic, pushed open its creaky door, rummaged through bygone steamer trunks, plastered with decals of former travels. Hanging inside were forgotten clothes, waiting for every flight of fantasy; torn feathered hats, frayed silken gowns, high buckled boots—stiff and scented with old perfumes and mildew smells. Trays-of-trinkets and drawers-that-stuck awaited my daring, my imagination.

How I danced to the sun and the moon and the stars!

"I'm a giant butterfly! A butterfly with crystal wings!" I would shout to the silent walls. Wrapped in faded pink chiffon, I twirled around and around, lost to the world.

Sometimes playmates shared my drama, my theatrical ways. Usually my sister stayed apart, huddled in the darkest corner. For each friend, being of a different nature, these games were scary and make-believe. For me, they were no less real than "real life" itself. Spinning tales that held each speechless, I could captivate them for hours. They would close their eyes and listen, while we voyaged to lands faraway, seeking stars upon which to sit. Other times we pressed closer together, pretending to be creatures from outer space, "little green people" with pointed ears and shiny fingernails that tapered long and narrow.

Yet my friends became frightened when they saw colored sparkles in the air and shimmering blue lights around each other. My sister curled into herself and whimpered, too terrified to move.

"We're witches! We're witches, beckoning evil spirits!" they cried, clutching each other tightly.

But I tried to touch the lights, to see if I could catch one in my hand.

Often my brother spied on us. Claiming we were devil-playing, he aroused my parents' anger. Then, controlled and patient, Mother would appear. Offering afternoon tea and honey cakes, she pretended not to know what we were doing. She bristled from our games, disliked our playing with imaginative realms.

Anything you could not see or touch was suspect.

When everyone left, she would make me feel black and awful. Scolding me for frivolous thoughts, she tried to bring fear into my heart.

To stop all feelings, I turned my body cold as ice, stiff as steel.

I pretended to roll my eyes to the back of my head and look straight through her. Then my teeth were tightly clenched. My ears closed, so no sound was heard. When her words ceased, only then did I return. It was a rhythm of fading-in and fading-out, floating away while she was angry. Sometimes I made her into the black sorceress of the night, or changed her into a wispy fairy godmother. Sometimes I drifted away on a carved river boat, or else wished for my Madame Alexander doll, waiting silently on my bed.

Yet, how had they chosen my perfect name? "Aisling" I was called—an ancient Celtic name meaning "vision or dream." The message behind the name eluded them, or so it seemed. They wondered whom I took after. Perhaps our eccentric aunt who kept crocodiles in her pool. Or that long forgotten cousin said to have been boiled in a pot in the African jungles. Any explanation would do.

As they couldn't fathom the inside of me, so they chose to groom the outside.

But nothing succeeded. Never were they satisfied.

I tried my best to please them, kept my bedroom tidy, did my schoolwork well, brushed my hair a hundred strokes.

Yet meal times told the truth.

None of us could finish what the maid served from the silver platter. Before breakfast began, last night's dinner had to be eaten. We learned to hide food in our pockets, and threw up many a meal. Without our feelings being heard, how could we stomach our world? I became a plastic doll in a yellow smocked dress, my sister a baby with ready tears, my brother a demon in disguise.

My escape was into the fantasy world.

There all was magic and light.

Imaginary friends cherished me, fairies in the breeze, calling my name, tapping each shoulder with a golden hand, blowing puffballs into silken strands, tempting me with spiral castles and mysterious keys. But, sadly, they vanished with every afternoon sun, leaving me to the loneliness of my bedroom.

In wintertime the fairies disappeared, for they were children of sunshine. Then frost and winds kept me home, entangled in the household maze. The changing cook and nagging nurse, the parlor maid and Edward, all watched me with suspicious eyes. Sometimes, when Mother was coming, I hid beneath the dining room table, hoping she might find me.

That was the only game I played with her.

The rest was education and etiquette.

Father, gentle and remote, remained locked in a world of silence. His position was second-in-command. With her cat-brown eyes, Mother held unquestioned authority. Little laughter, but many tears, passed between them. Caught by her hypnotic beauty and erratic temper, no one challenged her words. Whom the lioness would strike next, we never knew.

Everyone tiptoed through the house.

Yet Father held position in the outside world. His books about ancient cultures were stacked on library shelves. At home he played the child, being taken care of, like the rest of us. Any decision, as long as he did not have to make it, was fine. That was his means of escape.

Yet for me his presence was comforting. Whenever we were together, he never corrected my ways. He found something kind to say, or gently placed his hand upon my head. Often I wandered into his study, seeking his company, searching among his rows of dusty books. Usually he was there when I entered the room. He would raise his blue-grey eyes to look over his silver rimmed glasses, smile, then return to writing.

The fire was always crackling on a winter's day. I would snuggle into the velvet armchair, read his childhood books, all yellowed and scribbled with curious thoughts. How often I stared into the leaping flames, watching "faces" come and go, mesmerized by the fiery colors and hissing sounds. It was during one of these peaceful times, nestled before the shining embers, that I met a friend.

It all began with a voice I wasn't sure I heard, then a phrase here and there, then short sentences. It was unlike the fairies calling me. We had spoken without words. This voice seemed *inside* my head. I couldn't tell when or why the sounds would come. It always happened when I was dreamy, aware of "empty thoughts," my mind anticipating the unexpected.

At first it was amusing, then intriguing. I strained to hear what was said. Usually it began with someone calling, "Aisling, Aisling, Aisling!" I would turn around, but no one was there. Sounds repeated themselves, then little sentences formed, until the tone became clearer.

I called this voice "Whisper" and soon recognized his ways.

Becoming more curious, less timid, I awaited instructions. The forest became another world. My fairy friends watched as Whisper showed me birds and everything that moved, listening to the soft rustling of leaves. The woods held a special enchantment, now silent as a green cathedral, now alive with tiny voices and scurrying movements in the undergrowth.

Yet even at the quietest moment I was no longer alone.

Always at hand was my new friend Whisper.

His voice became as close as my shadow.

"Come," he would tease, "let's find butterflies hiding in dewdrops!" Or, "Quick! Quick! Mushrooms are growing by moonlight!"

And he would watch as I, Aisling, unable to resist temptation, left whatever I was doing to seek adventure.

And adventure it was indeed!

All paths led to the heart of the forest.

Breathless from running, hair flying in the wind, I listened for Whisper's voice. He showed me a spider's lace hammock for swinging, the pond's silver leaf for sailing, clumps of toadstools opening like padded umbrellas. And when I felt hungry there were nuts to nibble and tea laid out on the rocks.

Whisper guided me through this magical world, leading me deep into the ways of mystery. Soon I followed the flight of the dove, found trees with tinkling chimes inside, wove through the fabric of the forest.

Yet Whisper kept repeating one sentence I didn't understand.

"Aisling," he would say, "the woods and your rambling house are blown by the same wind."

"But why tell me this?" I asked.

"For the day you question what you have seen!" came the cryptic reply.

And no more was ever said.

Now that I was "outdoors," Mother had ceased to question my activities. Fresh air was synonymous with health. Radiant rosy cheeks pleased her. But Father was supicious. His curious smile wondered what I was doing. As usual, he observed rather than spoke, keeping all thoughts to himself.

Exhausted with excitement, each night I fell into a deep sleep. Reliving every moment of the day with all its magic, I awaited tomorrow.

Yet things happened only when they weren't expected.

II

The Awakening

NIGHT TIME became as exciting as day.

When the sun slowly faded and the light disappeared, another world unfolded. It was time to say good night and go upstairs. There, cocooned beneath my silk coverlet, I snuggled as nurse read a fairy tale, kissed me on the forehead, turned out the bedside lamp. Through my window I watched the carpet of stars lay across the evening sky. I pretended the whole earth was sleeping as well.

At first tiredness made me feel heavy.

Then lightness came.

Falling asleep had a rhythm of its own, a gentle drifting into the arms of darkness, a sensation of falling into another space. During these moments the lightness became as soft as a falling leaf.

It was then my vivid dreams began.

Sometimes there were the horrors of the night; leery black bears would prance wildly about, enticing me into their whirling dance; iridescent snakes, wearing my brother's face, twisted around my legs, dragging me into thickening quicksand; a deep eddy caught me in its sucking vortex, while kicking and screaming I tried to free myself from its clutches.

No one ever heard my cries. Nurse was drowned in snoring.
And my bedroom was at the far end of the house.

But there were lovely, magical dreams as well.

One returned many times. I never knew when it would appear. It mystified me.

I stood alone in a bleak, windowless, empty room. In the right-hand corner appeared a heavy wooden door with animal carvings and a glistening brass knob. The door was half-ajar. From a safe distance I would study this door, curious where it might lead but hesitant to explore, despite the golden light that shone through its opening. On one occasion a Silver Bird swooped down onto the crystal floor. His emerald eyes caught my glance. But the beaming ruby in his forehead, flashing brightly whenever I looked up-wards, was even more compelling. The bird summoned me to follow him. I did not move. I sensed that beyond the golden light was empty space—a vast hole from which I might not return.

Little by little I moved away from the dream.

But it haunted me, made me restless.

I decided to forget my fright and walk through the door should the dream appear again.

And recur it did.

That very night.

Almost at once I heard Whisper's voice.

"The path, the path, follow the path!" he urged.

"How can there be a path in light?" I asked.

But Whisper did not reply.

When shyly I opened the door, I found myself facing a second door, and when that opened, yet another. I moved cautiously through them, feeling lost as everything changed size—each door stretched taller while I shrank smaller. And then the Silver Bird, who had been following, grew so large his shadow positively dwarfed me.

Bewildered, I turned to the silent bird for comfort.

At least he seemed a friend.

Gently arching his back, he spread his wings, welcoming me within his silken folds. No sooner did I relax than lightning streaks flashed and crackled. "Help! Help!" I cried. But it was too late. The bird was lifting off the ground, sailing me into the depths of the night.

There were no stars around, only blue-violet light and deep silence.

Through this dusk the Silver Bird carried me to a jasmine scented garden, fluttering with the wings of a thousand humming-birds. Brilliant colors bombarded me. To be within their fireworks was frightening.

I longed to be somewhere else.

In that instant of doubt, vultures attacked where there had been song. Now a vicious crow with beady eyes, the Silver Bird charged at me. I cowered, tried to hide into myself. Closing my eyes, I prayed for everything to disappear. In desperation I even pleaded for the Silver Bird to return. Instantly he appeared, lifted me once again, as if nothing had happened.

Next I remember hugging my pillow, shaking with fright, confused yet fascinated, not knowing what to do.

So it was that my first dream journey began.

In my daytime "real life," I wandered around, dazed. Nothing satisfied me, nothing comforted my unease. I needed to be alone. My mind played tricks, dividing my thoughts and feelings. 'Angry me' wished I had never touched that magical door. 'Curious me' longed to see the Silver Bird again.

One thing was certain—until it made sense, my dream remained a secret.

Many nights later the Silver Bird reappeared, waiting for me to climb onto his back. I decided to be his friend. Together we sailed the indigo sky and watched the stars awaken. Each moving light, bursting into color, rang with unfamiliar chords. Harp music surrounded everything gliding through space. All around, as we flew through the mystical night, invisible beings with honeysuckle scents drifted by, sprinkling the air with sweet perfume.

But what followed this heavenly music and enticing fragrance, I never knew, for the further I flew with the silent bird, the less my waking mind retained.

My dream memory became hazy.

Only vaguely did I remember floating through strange lands with transparent trees that slowly moved. Tantalizing fragments of these journeys came back to me—entering tunnels with startling lights at the end of them; flying through midnight spaces at precarious angles; touching silvery metallic surfaces that fleeted by.

Always there was Whisper to reassure me.

"Aisling, look to lands faraway," he said softly, "for you are seeking stars once known!"

Then even this memory faded.

When morning came I would lie in bed, perplexed, wondering where I had been during the night. It was then I felt suspended, neither "in" nor "out" of my body. Several minutes passed until I felt comfortable in my physical self. I decided that that was "real."

Visions were just my imagination.

"Perhaps they will go away," I thought.

Instead, the dreams accelerated.

One unforgettable morning I awoke abruptly, upset to find my body chilled, my nightdress damp. Cold air had entered the bedroom yet no window was open. All about was a frozen stillness. Too dazed to call my nurse, I did not move.

Instead, I clutched my silk coverlet and waited for something to happen.

And happen it did!

Before my startled gaze, the bedroom slowly flooded with golden light—the same radiant light I had seen beyond the door in my dreams.

Then the windows swung gently open.

My ears began to ring with a high-pitched sound.

Whisper kept silent, for something wonderful was beginning to emerge from this golden warmth.

Breathless, I witnessed a dream come to life. Before my astonished eyes, a Mystical Being took shape. I reached out, tried to feel his shimmering silver robes, touch his dazzling crown, see if his brilliant diamonds were real.

But my hands met only air. What looked solid was made of light!

The vision was floating on nothing, drifting within a throbbing glow.

Perhaps I was sleeping still, awake within my own dream. Pinching my cheeks proved foolish. The vision would not go away. He just beamed towards me, penetrating my feelings with thoughts, leaving me exposed. His silvery eyes shone with the coolness of the moon, his presence filled the room with indescribable love and warmth. Through the silent air, the vision floated in stardust waves. Then suddenly everything stilled.

Spellbound, I could not move.

"Speak up! Speak up!" urged Whisper.

The words that stumbled from my mouth were hesitant.

"Please, please . . . Who are you? . . . Where do you come from? . . . Why are you here?"

But the visitor spoke not a word.

Instead, thoughts streamed from his mind towards me.

"You, my child, are in the twilight zone, neither awake nor asleep. The abode of no time, no space, no memory, no place. And I am yet unknown."

Little of this did I understand.

Yet it didn't seem to matter.

I found myself drifting into the rainbow colors floating from the visitor's thoughts. Each sentence rode a colored light beam, each word glittered alone.

Being so fascinated, my fears were forgotten.

"There are wondrous things to come," the Mystical One continued. "Worlds of delight hidden in spirals of eternity! Winding paths leading to celestial kingdoms await your arrival. Only first, there are lessons to be learned, obstacles to surmount, knowledge to become wisdom. For inner worlds open to those who overcome trials. Then does one love the thorn as well as the rose."

"But why have you chosen *me*?" I asked.

"For you have heard my voice before!" came the reply. "Now I have come to bestow the Cape of Flying. Your precious cloak will be rainbow blue satin lined with white dove feathers. Blue gives comfort and vitality in times of need. White feathers lighten one's burden, bringing joy and laughter. Open wide your satin wings as you travel to stars beyond. Far-memory will return once again!"

The Mystical One smiled at me, an awe-struck girl in her bed.

"Now I must leave," he murmured. "I shall return when you know those who inhabit the White Light. My role is to wait and watch, guide and protect, but never interfere. After you have gone

17

through crystal mirrors to worlds unknown, then shall I find you again.''

With that, he vanished.

I was left dumbfounded, yet ecstatic.

Then I realized *my* body was light and floating as well!

Intense sound, buzzing all around, prevented my dozing. Unable to resist the whirling rhythm, I began to gently sway and rock. Whisper wanted me to know this was not the drifting feeling before sleeping. Rather, it was my second body freeing itself.

He waited, watching me experience this dream-self float towards the ceiling.

It was peculiar, even frightening.

I could look down and see ''Aisling'' on the bed. I could look up and see ''me'' hovering above. In that instant, seeing myself in two places at once, I became terrified. The second body began to contract into my physical self.

''Float, Aisling! Drift with your dream-self!'' commanded Whisper. ''FLY! FLY! FLY!''

Obedient, I sank as if in sleep, let myself go.

My second body bumped into the ceiling without coming to harm, moved in and out of closed windows, flew through shut doors, even safely returned. From this air-view, everything seemed easy, effortless. Feeling brave, my spirit-self started to venture into the countryside.

But a strong pull prevented this.

It was from my physical body. As if awakening from slumber, it beckoned my dream-self to return. No longer did it have the energy to support my flight.

Instantly the second body returned home.

I fell asleep while trying to remember what had happened.

Yet, something bothered me. Was this "real" or just "a dream within a dream"?

And whom could I ask?

III

The Rainbow Quest Begins

FOR SEVERAL NIGHTS THEREAFTER my dream body and physical body continued to separate. It no longer frightened me, nor took me by surprise. At first I only dared to fly within the room. There was something about hovering on the ceiling, looking down upon myself in bed, that was awesome.

And too many questions still lingered. Who was the radiant visitor? Was it *he* who caused my dream body to fly? Would the Mystical One return again?

So much was so strange, how could I tell my parents? Surely they would claim it was my imagination, make-believe land again. They would watch me more carefully than ever. This way I held the memory as my truth, crystal clear and unclouded.

A private world of "secrets" became mine. Many hours drifted into daydreaming, reliving every detail of the visitation, an old movie seen over and over again. Denying the experience seemed futile, and rethinking the scene made it more difficult to recapture, for my memory played tricks. Yet, as the remembrance slowly faded, my yearning for the Vision grew stronger. Like sand slipping through my fingers, so my frustrations began.

This new loneliness made me restless, impatient, agitated. Its memory could not be understood in the usual way. Too insecure to share my thoughts, I sought the comfort of solitude. I read and re-read books about apparitions, ghosts, strange happenings.

Still nothing satisfied my questions.

The search became an obsession.

Whisper tried coaxing me back to the forest.

"Come, Aisling," he would say, "daffodils are dancing with daisies, tulips are talking to turnips!"

I paid no attention. My constant thought was the silent, magical speech of the Vision of Light. In comparison Whisper seemed trivial.

"Aisling," he insisted, "the woodlands are waiting for you!"

Only then did I agree to go.

And when I did return the forest was different. Or, was I the one who changed?

It seemed another place.

Wandering between the darkness of the trees, following a voice within my head, I came upon an unexpected clearing. There stood a cottage, one I had never seen before. It was small and thatched, perfect as a doll's house, surrounded by a tiny garden of cultivated flowers and shaped hedges. Its neatness contrasted with the wildness of the woods.

It even had a white picket fence, no higher than my waist. I peered over it, surprised to find painted gnomes, stone mushroom stools, dwarfed fountains, half-hidden in the grass.

Nurse's fairy tales loomed in my mind.

Again I had the sensation of not knowing where I was.

"Good morning, child!" a chirpy voice startled me.

The sound of the voice shattered my daydream.

Standing at the cottage door was a plump, gray-haired, spectacled lady, hands tucked in her apron pockets. There was not a wrinkle on her kind face, nor a line of worry. Soft blue eyes and rosy cheeks smiled together.

She looked to be everyone's perfect grandmother.

"Oh, good morning," I said hastily, suddenly feeling awkward, for surely it was afternoon.

A short, disconcerting silence followed, but the old lady took no notice and kept smiling.

"My, my, how you've grown!" she finally said, making me feel further out of touch.

My sensible part wanted to leave this funny old woman and her tidy cottage, but the curious part rooted me to the spot.

Still, she seemed harmless enough, perhaps in need of a friend.

For no reason I switched to thinking about tea, chocolate cake, honey, biscuits, and found myself walking inside the cottage. There was a breeze blowing from behind, directing where I was going. It was not at all surprising to find the table set for two.

No sooner had I sipped some tea, than my eyes were drawn upwards, espying a little Silver Bird. It was hovering near the ceiling, fluttering in the air. Its resemblance to the bird of my dream was astounding.

The old lady kept chattering away, telling me about the forest—which berries could be eaten, which were poisonous, of insects following the patterns on flowers into their hidden nectars.

Half of my mind fixed on a "friend" above my head; the rest studied the old woman, watching her movements, wondering whom she was. An uneasiness came upon me. Was this person before me real, another dream, a witch in disguise? Was I trapped in some fantasy, or free to leave? Was a magic spell being woven around me?

Everything was too good to be trusted.

At that very moment the tea table began shaking, dishes clattered, jam flew everywhere. A huge chasm had opened in the floor—pulling me into it! I was falling to the bottom of the earth! Roaring winds of confusion blew through my mind. From every direction darted black shadows and fang-toothed demons. Taunting voices mocked me.

Just as I turned upside-down, screaming, my dress blowing wildly about, the old woman's hand reached out and rescued me.

Shaking from head to toe, I held onto the chair. *What* was going on? I needed some explanation for this horror.

The old woman just smiled. She gave me tea with herbs to calm me down. Her detachment puzzled me.

"One who seeks the Light attracts the Dark," she said at last. "Let that be a warning, child. Creatures of blackness feed on fear. And the fear of doubt opens the darkest doors."

The Silver Bird flickered before my eyes, looked straight at me, then vanished.

"Perhaps you have found the right place," the old woman continued, "but refuse to recognize the signs."

How was it that words started pouring from me?
Loosened by fright, I began speaking my most hidden thoughts.

Secrets fell from my mouth. Did she know about flickering blue lights? Had a golden hand ever touched her shoulder? Had her name ever been called when no one was there? Did she see lights glowing around people, shining like fireflies in the night? Had she seen faces change in size and shape and age, with headdresses of different times?

While I babbled away, the old woman just went on nodding and smiling.

"There are no accidents, my child," she said, when I had exhausted myself. "Things happen as they are meant to. All of us ' see' but some ' see' more than others. There are worlds waiting for those who look!"

Then I spoke of the songs in trees, the soft murmur of roses held to my ears, of waves in seashells, of the sounds in growing grass.

The old woman just smiled.

"You will be alone, Aisling, but never lonely," she said, gazing out the little window framed by pink geraniums.

She offered another cup of tea.

"No, no, thank you," I said, suddenly anxious. "It's time to be going home."

Which wasn't entirely true.

The forest was calling. It was foolish to have pretended otherwise. The old woman could read my thoughts.

She took no notice.

"Some things belong to the silent world," said the old lady, placing her arm around me. "Cherish what you 'see' for few know of dimensions between worlds. Those who find the way, respect its code of silence."

She waved goodbye, telling me to come again, anytime.

Once again, breezes pushed me from behind. I found myself drawn to the dark forest. But, being excited, I became over-anxious. The more I desired what I couldn't "see," the more the fog rolled in. I lost the rhythm of the birds.

"Serenity awakens sleeping flowers," Whisper said and then repeated it again and again.

Often I liked what he said. And sometimes he simply annoyed me. I wondered *where* Whisper came from. Yet, in spite of my resistance, he usually was right. He sensed where I should be going and paid little attention to where I was stuck.

Not knowing what else to do, I stared at a leaf, pretending to be inside. Whisper watched me enter its maze of transparent, hexagonal cells. Swishing noises moved me about like a bee in its honeycomb. Next I listened to rocks, heard pulsing sounds. Diamond lights danced in the air. These were temptations on the way.

But I had to learn to be silent and listen.

All this "wanting" had made me tired.

I rested beneath a tree. Shadows were forming between leaves, dusk was coming. Soon I must leave for home. The branches above me hummed with music, each leaf became a word. Was I imagining voices again?

This time I stayed alert.

"Look here! No, there! No, here again!" I thought I heard.

Then songs filled the air.

Come find me, oh find me, child of the dream.
A voice is the shadow, wings are the stream.
Your hair is the stardust, your feet are kept bare.
Come quickly, young maiden, and seek if you dare!

A web of spiral rainbows spun around me. For a moment the trees melted before my eyes. Then, from a distance, trumpets sounded:

"'Tis for you," the spirits sang, "the forest beckons you forth!"

My waiting had come to an end.

28

Just as the Vision of Light had foretold, the call of the Quest was upon me.

Abruptly, as it started, so everything stopped.

Anxiously, I looked about.

Where there had been breezes, now came the wind. It turned me around, ushered me home.

The test of silence had begun. Yet who would believe my tale?

Mother might scold me. Father, fond of facts and logic, would tolerate my childish rantings. What if nurse wanted to see the old woman's cottage? How would I ever find it? Only Whisper knew the way. And how could I tell about *him*? My brother would relish the chasm of demons—but what if he acted it out?

My mind was turbulent.

After a sleepless night, a decision was made. My secret would not be shared. Nothing was going to stop me.

Greeting the dawn with excitement, taking care not to awaken anyone, I slipped from the house into the first cool light. Quivering, I reached the edge of the trees.

But how was I traveling? In my physical body or dream body? I could not answer that question, not yet.

"Follow invisible lights," Whisper urged.

Anxious to find what I couldn't "see," I obeyed.

Neither fairies nor elves nor gnomes greeted me. The nature spirits, curious about my new movements, stayed silent. Our games belonged to another past. From the moment the Quest began, time had lost its meaning and events were being shaped by a presence still unknown.

Asking no questions, I was guided without words. High-pitched noises and dashing lights surrounded me. White owls peered through thickened trees. An eagle fluttered above my head. Tiny flowers shook off the morning dew.

An unfamiliar stream caught my eye. I followed its course.

It led to a clearing of fairy-ring mushrooms. Here was a place of magic, clustered with crystalline butterflies. My fairy friends were weaving a circle of dance, slipping in and out of each other, pretending surprise to see me. Where one began and another ended, I couldn't tell, for their lavender raiments fused together. To my astonishment they drew the stream's water into their ring, forming a small but perfect pond.

A voice I had heard before now greeted me again. Then I saw the Rainbow Spirit glimmering before me.

> *You have found me at last, child of the dream,*
> *By tracing the path of our magical stream.*
> *So come to me child—you have nothing to fear,*
> *If you think about 'there' you are suddenly 'here'.*

In a twinkling I was inside the pond, tightly clutching the hand of the Rainbow Spirit.

I gasped. "How can I breathe? . . . What if I swallow water? . . ."

But we were diving too fast for the Spirit to hear.

Racing through swirling waters, we were sucked into a glistening spiral, which twirled us around and around, until we arrived on an island covered entirely with red rose petals.

"Say something! Say something!" Whisper commanded. "Aisling, do not hesitate now!"

"Where am I? Why have you brought me?" I stammered.

The Rainbow Spirit acknowledged my fright and explained.

> *You have traveled far, the time draws near,*
> *For us to share what we hold most dear.*
> *Our teachings are hidden and given to those*
> *Who follow the vision and find the rose.*

Our lessons are many, the tests prove severe.
You have chosen the way, the path is now clear.
We shall give you a gift of immeasurable worth,
By showing the Rays that govern your Earth.

But surest of all, you will learn about YOU,
'Tis your mirror reflection we'll hold up to view.
So see yourself clearly, dare not to look back,
That is our warning: there is only one track!

Then the strong north wind, summoned by the Rainbow Spirit, scattered red rose petals everywhere. Their sweet fragrance deceived me. Layer upon layer fell upon me, suffocating me until I felt my fright.

"Where am I? Where am I?" I cried again, trying to free myself from this surging mass of Red.

"You have reached the bowels of the Earth, the source of Eternal Flames," Whisper declared.

How could Whisper, my friend, do this? How could he lead me to fire, my worst nightmare? One horrible dream began to repeat itself—the one of my Father and brother dragging me through the scorching flames. Shaking with fear, while Red expanded more and more, I tried to stop the throbbing of its burning embers.

Soaring flames were all around.

They had captured the beautiful Rainbow Spirit!

Instantly, she melted away.

And I was left alone, too terrified to move.

IV

The Dance of Fire

SPELLBOUND, I WATCHED the Spirit of Red emerge from the dreaded flames. His appearance frightened me. My instincts were not to meet him. Feverish from the scorching heat, I searched for a place of refuge. But the scalding walls closed in on me. Stalactites and stalagmites cast ominous flickering shadows. Red clay steps led deeper and deeper into the crackling flames. My ears buzzed with high-pitched ringing. Was this a warning to stay or leave?

Delirious and lost, staring into the flames, I begged the Rainbow Spirit to return. The only sign received was a burst of rainbow colors flickering, then disappearing into the flames.

It was an unsatisfactory answer to my prayers.

Once more I looked about. Waves of glassy heat now shimmered through the air. The soil beneath my feet began to move. Losing all sense of space and time and weight, I seemed to see crowds before me, tense people in somber robes huddled together, fears and whispers spreading amongst them. Were they staring horrified at *me* burning on the stake, praying for the torment to end? Or was it a saint, a witch, a thief, an adulteress before their frightened eyes?

33

Terror seized my heart. Again, the memory of dying in leaping flames haunted me. How many nights I awakened screaming, burning in the dream of fire.

Was I born with this fright?

The only comfort from fire came when gazing into a safe fireplace, watching pictures come and go. In the nightscape of dreams terror arose. How often I dreaded going to sleep. One of these visions, familiar from darkness, now faced me again.

In a pastoral landscape of rolling hills and cloudless sky, I saw myself in the clutches of a monstrous dragon with bloodshot eyes and blood-filled claws. Flames spewing from his nostrils, he was attacking my knight in silver armor. As the land beneath us buckled, fire spread amongst the trees. When my knight's sword pierced the dragon's flesh, I shrieked.

My fright proved stronger than my faith.

Fear caused the vision to vanish and nothing was resolved.

My body wanted to run in any direction—to cry in nurse's lap, pick up daisies in the field, hide in the comfort of my little room.

The Spirit of Red stopped this means of escape.

Through a pathway of blazing torches, he strode towards me.

Startled by his energy, my mind went blank and for a moment I forgot my alarm. Hypnotized by his magnetic eyes, thoughts of leaving vanished. Close to me, the Spirit seemed splendid, dynamic, alluring.

His scarlet cape, flung open to adventure, was clasped by rubies so bright that flames flickered in them. A transparent garment sculptured his powerful form. Its starkness embarrassed and excited me. My face flushed. Mother would have rushed me away in haste, lest my innocence be tainted.

But I drew closer.

His daring and vitality, his brashness, swiftness and skill, lifted my spirits. No one at home was ever like this! Trouble suddenly seemed appealing.

I stared, mesmerized by the Spirit's ember eyes, his bronze-red skin, his opened hands that beckoned in temptation. Before his commanding ways and forceful desires, I felt young and hesitant. I began looking at him, and through him, at the same time. Was this yet another haunting spell? For he was changing, chameleon-like, before my astonished eyes—sometimes almost human, sometimes the ghost of a warrior, sometimes light as air.

He cared little for my gaping.

Familiar with the game of conquest, he turned from me to seek some other audience. Taking a wide stance, proudly flashing his golden goblet, he toasted, sipping red wine between dramatic words.

"Before all I praise man's carnal desires," he exclaimed, raising the goblet higher and higher, "his willpower and lust, his prowess, his earthiness!"

"What *are* you talking about?" I cried.

But the Spirit continued speaking as if I were not there.

> *Watch me and hear me and speak of me not,*
> *My flames are voracious, my temper roars hot!*
> *The body you sleep in concerns me the most,*
> *It feeds me and keeps me, for I am its host! . . .*

"I don't understand a thing you're saying!" I interrupted.

Abruptly, the Spirit turned towards me. Arrogance had replaced excitement. Being self-engrossed, he simply had forgotten my existence.

"Where am I? Why am I *here*?" I asked.

"And why, pray tell, are you here?"

"I have come on a Quest," I blurted.

"A Quest? A Quest? A Quest for what?" snapped the Red Spirit.

"To find the Mystical One, the source of all Light," I timidly replied. "He visited me in the twilight zone and told of my search to come . . . but . . . he never mentioned *you*."

"I, young lady, am the *first ray* one meets! I am the RAY OF RED!" came the curt reply. "Are you ready to follow *my* command?"

"Oh. . . . No! No! No!" I cried, panic rushing through me.

Once again, I wanted to get out of this inferno.

Where was Whisper, my eternal friend?

Did *he* dissolve in danger?

"Wipe your butterfly brow, Aisling," came his familiar voice. "Neither angels nor ants can help you now. Trials and temptations have begun!"

"Some friend," thought I, feeling faint from heat. My dress was so damp I could wring it out. My hair so wet water dripped from it. I could even taste salt droplets running down my cheeks.

"You're *still* thinking Earth-terms," said Whisper. "Here flames don't burn, fire does not scorch!"

Perhaps he was right.

Nothing was ignited but my mind.

And that was burning hot.

Suddenly the drama before me expanded. Iridescent salamanders, ten times taller than myself, caressed the flames. Guardians of Fire, they chanted, fanned its embers, excited its sparks. Their music reached a crescendo of such high pitch, my ears vibrated.

As the flame's height increased, I was reduced to the size of a pea. I had to stretch my neck to see the Spirit of Red. He was breathing vitality from the fire, as casually as one smells a rose! Becoming more aggressive, wildly pacing to and fro, he now shouted his worth, his masculine strengths.

I laughed with relief for he was toasting the world!

> *I'm dynamic and thrustful, I drive and inspire,*
> *Encouraging PASSION and HEAT and DESIRE!*
> *Red irritates, agitates, calls men to arms,*
> *For power and sex are its tokens and charms . . .*

This time I laughed aloud.

The flaming eyes looked down at me in anger.

Seeing that his audience of one was rebelling, the Spirit of Red reduced in size. Calmly, he tried to explain himself better.

"Are you not aware," he said, "that WE are Man's first teachers? The Earth is a University with lessons to learn. Having descended from Spirit to Matter, your world is solid and physical. Other kingdoms are shapeless, some invisible, some have no substance at all. From RED you will discover the secrets of Matter!"

"That doesn't surprise me," I commented, very grown-up indeed.

"Then how does Matter function and what is its purpose?" snapped my fiery tutor.

Before I could answer, he went on.

"I command the physical!" he shouted. "Endowed with the vigor of Mars, RED stimulates your heart, sets aflame passions and hungers. Your sports, your wars, your romances feed my every desire. I am your energy, your ambitions. With RED's blood you are powered, without it you perish!"

39

"Will you pledge your allegiance to my banner of Conquest, Power and Romance?" he demanded.

"What a foolish thing to ask me," I replied.

"Then you must suffer, little girl," came his fierce reply. "Those who do not heed my words walk through flames and step on red-hot coals!"

I cringed in horror at his volcanic passions.

"Note the excitement, that drama, the lava tongue!" teased my old friend, Whisper. "Was it not Daring and Courage that brought you here? Is not RED the breath of curiosity, the sunrise, the beginning of all beginnings?"

"What are you talking about?" I raged. Here I was filled with terror, and Whisper was expounding philosophy!

The Spirit of Red smiled his annoying, winning smile.

Around his head glowed the Red of dawn. From his hand shot a lightning bolt. It struck the earth before my feet. A pit gushing with molten lava boiled higher and higher, rapidly flowing towards my toes. Faint voices called me into the boiling liquid. The Spirit of Red stood by my side, breathing hotly, almost pushing me into the volcanic flow. His hands had turned to burning embers. I touched them and sizzling sensations ran through my blood.

Was this the Trial of Fire?

My head was throbbing, my ears buzzing, my feet and hands trembled. Without thinking, I started walking towards the pit. I was moving slowly, as if in sleep, towards the fiery lava. All nervous chatter stopped in my head. I had but one goal. I held my eyes steady on the chasm of fire and took the first step.

The Spirit's words rang in my head.

RED's help on your Quest is its positive drive,
It will shield you from danger and keep you alive.
For its strength is the COURAGE that waits in the
*   night,*
To lead you from darkness and out towards the Light...

His voice boomed loud and strong, shattering and splintering the cavern rocks into red hot sparks.

But *nothing* harmed me, not the boiling lava, nor the mounting flames, nor the singeing embers.

I was either out-of-my-body or out-of-my-mind.

I didn't know which—perhaps it was both.

Some instinct told me my physical body was still in the woods looking into the fairy pond. Another that I was sleeping in my bedroom. And my mental body? Why that was in the cottage of the old woman. Or was it somewhere else, dreaming new dreams?

My memory turned on itself. Confusion reigned.

Of only one thing was I certain, this land of fire was the shadow of an old dream. I remembered "seeing" that my dream body was made of Light sparkles. Of course, embers would not char my feet, nor fire burn my skin. Blazing flames made this body glow even more! Its warmth was like bubbles of fresh energy rushing everywhere.

Realizing this made me bold. My spirit felt freed from bondage. I began to whirl around and around the open pit, waltzing with the Spirit of Red, pretending to be the goddess of Fire, the princess of Flame.

As I spun deeper and deeper into the lava's vortex, the dance of Light whirled around me, for I had burned my nightmare and em-

41

braced my fright. I began to cry. Tears of joy and relief poured from my heart, releasing the fear of fire, trapped for a thousand years.

The Spirit of Red stared in disbelief, mystified by my clear state. He couldn't understand what he had done or said to change me.

"Perhaps," he said, "I should have given you the Kiss of Fire,"

But I was too involved in my own feelings to react. Nor did I notice my flood of tears dampening his flames. I didn't even see the Spirit of Red dissolve into the waters of emotion.

For I, Aisling, had collapsed, exhausted, into the sleep of tears, relieved to have ended the trials of RED.

V

The Orange Butterfly

I HAD CRIED SO HARD my eyelids seemed stuck together. Try as I might, I could not open them. All I could "see" was my "inner" screen, a dazzling show of rainbow colors and blinking sparkles with a reflection of myself inside them.

Had I become *one* with the dream?

For I was falling backwards in space, spiralling around and around, through billowy clouds, through deep sky, past twinkling stars. Each spiral turned slowly and gently. Streaming by, ever so swiftly, were orange shapes, cardboard pieces looking like magic carpets. Wide-eyed, I strained to see what they were. Swishing sounds followed hushed movements. Then I saw huge colored words shaded in every orange tint. Their sunshine glow was warm and tingling, like bathing in a hot summer wonderland.

Often two cards stuck together, magnetically drawn to one another. Yet many floated alone. Moving everywhere, falling upside-down and sideways, these strange cardboards flashed words before my astonished eyes: *Anger, Joy, Resentment, Depression, Rage, Laughter, Frustration, Hatred, Greed, Kindness, Sorrow, Arrogance, Generosity, Annoyance, Sadness, Cheerfulness, Hostility,*

Happiness—on and on and on fell the mysterious cards, naming emotions I never imagined existed.

How could I resist following them?

Twisting and twirling like them, it seemed as if the cards and I had fallen out of the sky. While floating softly downwards, the words "playing cards" flashed through my mind.

It could only be Whisper's hint.

But how had he found me?

"Stop thinking, Aisling, and try to feel. Stop watching and start experiencing!" he shouted. *"Emotions* are *Playing Cards* for the *Game of Life."*

I had no time to answer.

The flickering cards fell fast and furiously around me. Everything was coming alive! Now, I not only *saw* orange cards, but *heard* voices coming from them: arguing and fighting, bickering and crying, screaming and yelling, scolding and shouting. I wanted to cover my ears, stop these terrible noises. It was a symphony of sorrows.

Then I recognized one voice—my very own.

It was a voice from long ago. I was sobbing, terrified, certain I would die as an ether mask covered my face. Then I was screaming, slipping from a metal ladder, my leg torn and bloody. And that moving automobile—I was falling out of it, crying. And the ghost that walked my room at night! Why wasn't anyone listening? Why couldn't they *hear* my terror through the night? The vibrations pounded in my head, down my spine, into my toes.

The orange cards trembled with me.

I heard my parents quarrelling, the nurse and cook feuding, Edward trying to sing above the anger. Then I was in a temper tantrum, pillow pulled over my head, wanting my way more than anything else. Then came the sounds of war—bombs and gunfire and tanks—shrieks so loud my eardrums hurt.

Whatever was happening in one place was echoing elsewhere. Like a rolling snowball, event grew from event, and often the time was the same. Shouting my name, throngs of people answered. Was everyone in the entire universe calling one another? Soon I could not tell my voice from the others.

What was going on?

I tried to catch one of the orange cards.

But they flew past too swiftly.

I began to fling my arms wildly about, desperate to latch onto any passing card. And then, imagining myself on the shiniest card, I arrived where my thought had sent me. I slipped onto the card I had chosen.

Little did I know it was the Card of Tears.

It was wet and slippery, sobbing in many voices and tongues I could not understand.

Together we tumbled and turned, to where I knew not.

Except now the weeping I heard was mine.

Crying softly, as if in sleep, I had no recollection of what had caused this sadness. Exhausted, heavy with tiredness, I tried to open my eyes, thinking myself under the silk coverlet, dreaming a bad dream.

But I was not there.

Some stranger, tapping my shoulder, was trying to awaken me. An exquisite orange butterfly with tangerine wings was fanning me. No larger than my thumb, it had settled on my arm.

"What are you doing?" I asked. "And who are you?"

Not answering, it continued fanning and cooling my face. My head felt feverish, yet my hands touched my eyes instead. They were puffed and swollen and hurt. Then I remembered the flood of tears, my RED exhaustion.

"Look! Look!" laughed the tangerine butterfly. "Do you not see sweet tiger lilies beneath your feet? And fragrant orange blossoms awakening above your head? And the warm orange sun glowing before your reddened eyes?"

I blinked, hardly believing the scene before me. The grass was a picnic basket strewn with fruits of passion: mangoes, persimmons, apricots, oranges, peaches, tangerines. It was a feast to admire, but one I chose to devour. Famished, I attacked each one.

Nothing was what it seemed to be.

The ripe apricots, instead of satisfying, left me discontent. The luscious persimmons made me angry. Dark and depressed from the tangy oranges, I began imagining grotesque forms through the shadowy trees. As they came closer to me, my insecurities and doubts started again.

Stealthily I moved from the fruits, wondering if the butterfly was the devil in disguise. Why else was he arousing such emotions? Why did he want me discontent? Now, all I desired was to be alone, hidden in my bedroom, pillow pulled over my head, weeping, trying to control my disappointment and rage. Yet no one was going to see me this way! I remained unwilling to share my feelings. Better to grit my teeth and stay spiteful. That way I kept my distance. I wanted to run and run and run away from myself, away from others, away from the world.

To where I knew not.

No one offered the comfort I needed, no one understood my deepest resentments. The scene of sadness was familiar, safe and secure. I could anticipate my reactions, watch the pattern repeat itself over and over again.

47

"My, my, what self-indulgence, what self-pity, what lack of self-esteem!" said Whisper, amusing himself at my expense.

"Oh, do go away!" I said. "I'm sick of you, too!"

"Pride will only pamper you, anger will make you ugly!"

"Please, please, go away!" I repeated. "You're just as annoying as the others!"

Whisper obeyed and retreated. "Good," I angrily thought.

At last I was left to myself.

I had successfully chased everyone away, convinced that no one really wanted or needed me.

But a vast emptiness filled my body. Depressed, abandoned, fear welled up; my blood chilled, my eyes twitched, my throat became dry. I was sick again. This jungle of emotions was mine—was there *no* way out?

Desperation followed. Suddenly I wanted to find everyone I had sent away. In my irrational state I now longed for friendship, attention, tenderness, care. I stood before my own brick wall. I wanted to share with others, wondered what it would be like. Yet my longings were so vast only I could fill them.

Caught between my inner and outer self, only the grayness of doubt remained. But of one thing I felt certain. I needed to dance, sing and laugh with others, perhaps find mushrooms in the woods together, even walk through meadows picking wild flowers.

Torn between the solitude of my dreams, and wanting to be with others, I needed guidance.

"Please, please, Whisper—please come back again!" I pleaded.

But no sound was heard.

In the long silence, time felt weighted.

I withdrew, forgot the landscape around, lost all sense of reason. I made myself unreachable. My only true friend had vanished forever, no doubt to someone who loved him more.

48

Would I ever find him again?

I tried hard not to cry.

Instead, I looked around. Nothing had changed but my feelings. Birds were chirping, grass slowly growing, flowers opening their petals. Returning to the world again, my feelings began to unfold. One thought raced through my mind: *my moods* were out-of-sorts, nothing else . . . *my mind* was playing whatever games and tricks I allowed.

This idea was exhausting.

As I rested against an orange tree, its sweet blossoms and tempting fruits caught my attention. I touched its leaves and sensations of warmth returned. The tree was like a knowing friend. Its silence held neither rejection nor refusal. How could I retreat or run away? It "talked" to me, seeming almost human, soothing my battered feelings, offering comfort and strength.

"Take care, Aisling," fluttered the tangerine butterfly, "for what one asks for, comes to be."

He flapped his little wings, hinting of changes to come. Circling faster and faster around me, he became a warm, hazy blur. And, from this strange mist, once again emerged the gossamer wings of yet another Spirit.

"Welcome to ORANGE, my child!" laughed the Spirit, "through darkened clouds you found the glistening sun. How well our mirror played with your shadows and fears. What perfect echoes of YOU were the feelings you projected *around* yourself!"

"But I did nothing," I said, still convinced only fairies and magic mushrooms cared for me.

"Start loving yourself, then others will follow," suggested the Spirit.

49

I remembered my worried face at home, my seeking books instead of friends. With my fierce temper and sulky manners I found it easy to pretend I lived in a secret castle with alligator moats and a steel door no one could penetrate.

"Lift your drawbridge, throw away the rusty key!" encouraged Whisper. "Then see who comes to dine!"

"Oh, be my first guest" I smiled, grateful he had returned.

"True friends never leave," he said. "They wait until one has seen the light."

The Orange Spirit began fluttering her delicate wings, seeking my attention.

There seemed an urgency in her message.

Do nothing from excess, my child of the stream,
For heartaches and headaches will clog up your dream.
When free of emotional care and concern,
One's thoughts become opened and ready to learn!

"Because you overindulge your emotions, your body is exhausted," said the Spirit. "When the emotion of ORANGE is abused, then the strength of RED collapses."

I tried to defend myself but was given no chance to reply.

"There are neither excuses nor explanations on the Path. One must take full responsibility for *all* one's actions. Even *I* could not appear until you had found some inner peace. For in rage we see no one but ourselves."

Once more my attempt to say something was halted.

"That is *not* the way to learn," scolded Whisper. "Excuses do not erase errors."

"Trust yourself," said the Spirit, "know there are *no* mistakes, only lessons to learn. Worried emotions freeze and numb feelings, produce despair. Positive thoughts break all barriers."

"Look! Look!" she continued, holding a polished mirror. "See yourself as others see you. Reflections show what vision does not see. Fears form clouded minds and frozen hearts spread darkness. Happiness comes from open hearts, bringing lightness with it."

I saw the orange sun shining brightly through the mirrored glass. Thousands upon thousands of tangerine butterflies were calling me. Each butterfly flashed its complementary card: sharing and caring, giving and receiving, listening and speaking. From the blending of opposites, came the balance of emotions.

"Choose *any* cards," they laughed, "but are they not the *same?*"

Gently, my fingers touched each card. They no longer seemed opposed. Something had emerged from each confrontation—a new balance, a harmony not known before. No emotion held me more than another. There was no need to choose—only to accept the lesson before me.

The Orange Spirit, finding me clear again, my humor restored, fluttered her wings once more.

Except now, in poetic fashion, she was ushering me away.

She left me smiling, yet with a tantalizing farewell.

> *Waiting for you beside a road,*
> *With messages that need be told,*
> *Is a frog with silver winged sandals,*
> *And a daffodil of golden candles.*
> *The secrets they hide are for you to digest,*
> *So off with you, child, and on with the Quest!*

Then the Spirit spun light threads around me, enveloping me in a crystal egg.

I dared not crack its shell nor peer outside.

Closing my eyes, I decided to drift along and see where *it* would take *me*.

VI

The Yellow Cloud

"A FROG WITH SILVER WINGED SANDALS, and a daffodil of yellow candles . . . a frog with silver winged sandals, and a daffodil of yellow candles . . ."

These words kept spinning around in my head.

Trying to awaken and separate from the dream, I scratched my head, blinked my eyes. Then drew the bedcovers closer to my chin. Something peculiar had happened during the night, leaving weblike questions in my mind.

Again I rubbed my eyes, yawned, stared blankly at the ceiling. Curling my fingers around my hair, trying to remember, my frustration deepened. Surely the words meant something but . . . what, why, and for whom?

"Aisling, Aisling!" nurse called. "Where are you? Breakfast is being served!"

Quickly tumbling from bed, I dressed, left everything scattered, and hurried downstairs to the breakfast room. My eggs and toast were cold from standing. Everyone stared at me. No one said a word. Hoping to avoid a reprimand, I deliberately lowered my

55

head. Father glanced up from the newspaper, raised his eyes in disapproval. Mother took breakfast alone. Oblivious to others' thoughts, I silently ate my cardboard food, waiting to be excused.

I was in such a dream-fog, no one's judgment mattered.
But when mealtime finished, I didn't know where to go.
My thoughts were still in the maze of the night.
With my usual impatience, I wandered through the house.
"Try a frog, try a log, try a bog!" my mind foolishly suggested.
"Why not?" I answered.

And so I dashed towards the lake with its damp mud patches, secret holes, squeaky sounds.

Crawling on hands and knees, slippery leaves sticking to me, I stayed close to the water's edge. The silence of the hunt made me anxious. I jumped whenever frogs jumped. Their unexpected entrances and exits caught me off guard. Maybe it was better to watch them—their bulging eyes camouflaged behind wet leaves—than touch them. Anyway, weren't they all enchanted princes waiting to be freed from some wretched curse? Or could one be a phantom ghost, ready to capture *me* instead?

A deep-throated voice croaked near the rocks.

> *What thou seekest is a deadly curse,*
> *Caused by sins of darkness, yes, the very worst.*
> *Words used wrongly, thoughts to evil bent,*
> *Laziness of mind and tongue so useless spent.*
> *For this and more the plague is on my head!*
> *So THINK you well and lift me from the dead!*

Before I could dash away, the croaking continued.

Now if YOU miss this chance,
  to free the Prince of Thought,
Then may the curse be on YOUR head,
  and poison all you've sought!

"Who is speaking such words?" I whispered.

" 'Tis I, the Frog of Fate," came the reply. "Find me below the log, within the bog—hurry, quickly, for time draws near!"

But there was only a frightened frog. Wrinkled and wretched, he looked into my eyes. Carefully, I took him in my hands, stroked his head, watched tears flood his face.

"Oh, little frog, together we will try so . . . please no longer cry!" I brought him home, bedded on green moss, made him safe within a box. Nurse never suspected, tucked as he was in the darkest corner behind my bed.

But with him near my head, he never left my mind.

The theme of my dream became the frog.

Together we were caught in dreams within dreams within dreams.

I would watch myself watching him until I wasn't certain which was *me* and which was *he.*

Within every dreamscape loomed my friend, staring at me with his ugly warts and leathered skin. Bowing and smiling, sometimes he wore a foolish cap with silver wings, and sandals with the same funny things. Dressed so, he went dashing through the night sky, leaving trails of blazing light, gliding only in swift, straight lines.

Surely, I was going crazy.

"Only muddled people move in circles!" he shouted, tipping his hat. "There is another way than twists and turns!"

57

Thickness and fog surrounded me.
I understood nothing.

With silver wings streaking, my frog friend flew about, inspecting every speck of dust. He would watch it move, place it here and there, experiment, try again. What was he searching for? Was he thoughtful and reasonable, or completely mad?

"You are such a child!" he croaked in disgust. "Pay attention to the shifting sand, the darkened woods, the sleeping snail!"

"Then what happens?" I cried.

Now engrossed in his game of wonder, my friend continued flying from one thing to another.

No sooner did he *think* something, than it appeared. When his *thought* left, the object vanished as well. My dreamscape became a mass of flying matter; paper books, music scripts, tin cans, plastic combs, silver spoons, rubber boots, wooden tables, cars, pillows, bridges, bottles, ships, sandwiches. They passed by in a fury, leaving not a trace behind.

"I think you're *mad!*" I finally shouted.

"At last you're *thinking!*" he croaked. "Now try to *understand* what I'm doing, have *awareness* of what's before you, some *clarity* in your words."

Like scattered thoughts, the objects left me confused.

Until I realized *they* were part of *me.*

As objects fell, so one thought fell after another. Everything tumbled together. Perhaps *nothing* existed without *thoughts* about them.

Did thinking make things happen? Create new forms?

"Closer, closer!" called the frog. "Come and see within my tree!"

"You want me to look *inside* as well as *outside*." I laughed.

Like a faint voice calling from the past, I started to remember. Somewhere there was an *emptiness*. And into the emptiness, thoughts were put and forms pulled out—or—forms were put, and thoughts pulled out.

Everything seemed inside-out, even backwards, reversed and upside-down.

Was my *mind* creating all these *forms*?

Was it *me* who made my life?

My friend spun around me, swifter and swifter. At times he seemed an ugly frog, at times a Spirit carrying me through clouds of thought, past confusion into yellow brightness.

As I freed him, was he freeing me?

The cyclone was moving too fast.

Abruptly I ended the dream, held tight to the white linen sheets, stroked the "real" frog in the box. The "real" and "dream" worlds were getting too close. No longer was I certain of anything. I moved between awe and fear, wonder and fright.

Where was the balance I sought?

"Come, come, Aisling," laughed Whisper. "Have you forgotten? The daffodil of golden candles who follows silver winged sandals?"

"Oh, that!" I answered.

I had had enough of riddles.

"Trips of the *mind*, tricks of the *mind* are playing with Aisling today!" said Whisper.

But that driving force kept pushing me forwards. To stand still was impossible.

I relented.

"The daffodil's head is to be read!" hinted Whisper.

"But it makes no sense. . ."

"Relax, Aisling," came the reply. "You create your own reality—and that is what is before you."

"But. . ."

"There are no 'buts,' only a willingness to try."

Whenever I thought of daffodils, Mother came to mind. "Bite their stems between your teeth," she would say, before putting them into a vase. She often made statements without giving reasons. Just like Whisper. It made me feel left out. Then I would try to find the *reason* myself.

Was it from anger or curiosity that I wanted to know everything?

Only when emotions were involved, did my mind seem to change.

Now my stubborness had to be overcome.

For it was clear that Whisper meant another kind of daffodil.

"Tell her who I am." I next heard a voice command.

"No, not yet," Whisper answered, to my surprise.

"But the Prince of Thought is free and once again wears the sandals of Mercury!"

"She would not understand," Whisper replied.

"As Aisling helped me, so must I help her."

"With a messenger of the gods, I cannot dispute." And, with that, Whisper seemed to bow away.

Before me came this very Mercury, elegant and slim, moving with the speed of lightning.

"So that's what happened to my warty friend!" thought I.

Graciously, he swept towards me, delivered a single daffodil to my hand.

"Whatever you need, I shall come in the flash of a thought." He gleamed, waved his staff of twined snakes, and departed on silver wings.

I glanced at my prize, staring with hardly a blink. Ever so slightly, the flower's form began shifting. Its edges softened as in mist, then transformed into a shadowy candle. I kept my focus on the flame's blue light. Flickering softly, its light grew stronger and brighter. Concentrating on its center, my eyes seemed to stop moving. The candle disappeared completely, leaving a hazy afterglow, golden in tone. Then a being appeared, surrounded by flowers and fragrance, beckoning me to her.

It could only be the Spirit of Yellow!

"Well done, child! How skillfully you managed another mind-journey. Though you still don't know what it is or how it happens!" laughed the guide. "Soon it will be so natural you will move in and out of astonishing places with ease."

"Is that what the Quest is about?"

"Let us say other realms are lifting their veils. Come!" enticed my new companion. "Fly with me and see that what you *think* shapes you and your world!"

I hesitated. Being asked to fly was different from letting it just happen. Now I was responsible for my actions.

"Life is taking chances. Chances are changes," Whisper offered.

"But, what if. . ."

"No *buts*, only the willingness to try!"

The Yellow Spirit took my hand in hers.

"Won't you ask me 'who I am' or 'where I come from' or 'why am I here'?" she smiled.

"Well—I should like to know!"

She extended her other hand towards me.

"YELLOW is the messenger of Mercury, ruler of communication. Your thoughts, ideas, reasons, intellect, knowledge all come from us."

She snapped her fingers with authority.

Before me stood the man-of-swiftness, lean and graceful, his silver wings glittering brighter than ever.

"Here am I, your Prince of Dreams!" he teased me. "I have come to join your Thoughts and Feelings. For thinking with feeling brings the wisdom of gold."

"But will you vanish again?"

"My thoughts are always with you—you are never alone!"

"I know," I answered, discouraged. "Changes, changes, changes, changes, always changes."

"From thoughts come your actions and experiences," he said. "Take care to *say* how you *feel!*"

Again, he raised his face towards the sky, pointed straight ahead, disappeared with comet speed. This time I saw his silver wings turn to silver stardust.

"Communication reaches invisible and visible planes," comforted the Spirit of Yellow. "Fine magnetic threads connect *everything* through waves of energy. Come! I will show you!"

In a flurry of golden sparkles, we lifted off the ground, and soon were soaring into space. We floated above the Earth, staying close enough to see oceans, continents, white cloud patterns.

Below us, glistening in the sun, lay rolling wheatfields, rows of orchards, steel buildings, marble sculptures, landscaped gardens.

But now we were flying over war-charred lands, slums, cemeteries of cars, garbage strewn about—thoughts of destruction, neglect, ruin.

"Look how the mind can create or destroy," exclaimed the Ray of Yellow. "See the stale air your cities breathe. Fish are dying in your rivers and seas."

I saw the thick, grimy film hanging over most of the land. I recalled the dark shadow that clung to me when I felt weary, distrustful, neglected.

"All forms result from thought," said my Yellow guide. "Everything upon the Earth is *you!*"

"But how can that be?"

"Because one thought interacts with another. Minds together form ideas, then creations result. So your world shapes itself."

I hesitantly looked.

From where we were the Earth looked like an opal half-buried in grime and dirt. I wondered how much of myself was buried as well.

"Can we ever change things?" I shyly asked.

"Yes, through *clarity*," was the reply. "First you must know yourself, then be *aware* of your actions, then *understand* the results. *Think* from the crystal, but *act* from the heart!"

> *With that thought I leave you, all sunshine and bright,*
> *Remembering that HEART is the opening of SIGHT.*
> *You'll learn of this soon, as your travels unspin,*
> *For worlds are before you, they're yours just to win!*

After tapping my mind, the Yellow Spirit floated away.

I was astonished and fought back the tears. I was not ready to be stranded so far above the Earth. Without my guide beside me, my

63

head began to spin, then dizziness came. I couldn't even remember where my physical body was, no less my home.

I thought of my blue satin cape with white dove feathers.

It was for protection in times of need.

Wrapping it around myself, I settled on a fluffy cloud.

And waited.

VII

The Heart Land

My waiting seemed eternal. Sitting on a white cloud, hugging my Cape of Protection, I rested my cheek against the shimmering blue satin, cuddled into its warm dove feathers, and almost fell asleep in my own dream.

Then I sensed a presence nearby. Turning quickly, I beheld my beloved Rainbow Spirit.

"Where have you been? How did you ever find me?"

"I've been with you all along," smiled my secretive friend. "Now come and follow me!"

Remembering where this invitation had taken me before, I hesitated.

The Earth was far, far below us.

"I'm not certain I want to go," I replied, my stubborness asserting itself again.

"You got here quite safely, didn't you?" Whisper said reassuringly. "Try believing in those around you."

Reluctantly, I obeyed.

Yet I wished I had more say in these matters.

The Rainbow Spirit began spinning counter-clockwise around

me until I felt positively dizzy. As my body merged into the whirling vortex, I slid from the cloud, felt myself hurled into space. First there was a tingling buzz, then a whooshing-whirling sound. My body flooded with sensations, ripples of vibrations streaming from head to toe.

"There's little to be frightened of," confided the Spirit, sensing my unease. "Just relax and trust, fall gently as dust."

I was afraid to move—remembering too many dreams of falling, falling, falling, thrown from the cliff's edge, certain that death awaited me. In the vastness, unable and unwilling to relax, I always froze. I would awaken, a mummy, entombed in my own fears.

Why should this be different?

"First comes trust, then surrender," I heard Whisper say.

I tried to submit to the Rainbow Spirit, frightened as I was.

And the unknown was transformed into release instead!

As I dangled like a rag doll, my falling became fast and free. Somersaulting through the air, I twisted and turned, caught in a ringing sound. Now giddy and bursting with laughter, there was no stopping me.

As I became light as song, so my doubts dissolved.

The "ice cream cone" I had been spinning in, became narrower and warmer, until appeared a golden light.

"Are we here or there?" I finally cried, for the distance and dizzying speed had increased.

"Trust you must!" Whisper said again.

I wanted to object. Why was he always telling me what to do and feel?

Still this was not the moment for challenge.

We were travelling at too accelerated a speed, deeper and downward into the glowing cocoon. As the movement intensified, my chattering thoughts ceased.

I became weightless, light as Light!

Then, as if waking from sleep in surprise, we reached the cone's base and stopped abruptly.

The golden glow surrounding us slowly faded.

I blinked my eyes, thinking I *must* be in my dream, for I had been here many times before. The deep forest, the twisting road and rolling meadows, the awesome mountains and jewelled towers were scenes I already knew.

"Look at your feet." exclaimed the Rainbow spirit. "You are at least four inches off the ground! And *what* is holding you in place?"

Certainly I didn't know.

But it was all too true. My body was floating freely about, just like the Spirits themselves.

Everything around me was turning GREEN.

I yearned to reach the castle before dark. Which was most odd— because from here no castle was in sight!

"Can we hurry?" I asked excitedly. Even the sky was sequinned with green bubbles. The ground had started to move.

"Here we arrive when we think ourselves there. Neither light nor dark, time nor distance exist, only moving rhythms and changing waves," was the reply.

My sudden impatience caused us to fly.

We sailed through darkened trees, over winding paths and undulating valleys, passed green meadows without stopping, until the castle's towers were in view. The light around them was iridescent green, flickering with emerald sparkles. How many times I had been this close, but never this near to touch!

The enchantment was so engrossing that I hardly heard the Rainbow Spirit leave. Only when I realized I was on my own, did sadness overcome me. I had not even said good-bye.

"Never look back," Whisper murmured. "Gather the willpower of Red, the stillness of Orange, the clarity of Yellow."

And so I did.

Wrapped in my blue satin cape, I breathed a heavy sigh and floated towards the Kingdom, pretending I had visited many times before.

I was not prepared for what happened next.

Between the entrance towers blazed a laser-green light, so powerful and penetrating that I could not pass.

Nothing I tried succeeded.

"Don't *try*, let it *happen*." said Whisper.

My heart was pounding.

"Is . . . is someone around?" I asked.

"What do *you* want?" boomed a hearty voice.

"To enter Emerald Kingdom!"

"He who enters never leaves!" came the reply.

"Please, sir, please—have a heart."

"A heart, a heart, a heart!" he chuckled. "The heart of the matter is . . . now . . . what *did* you want, child?"

The Gate began to fade away. I feared my chance was lost. Keeping my heart open, I hoped it would return to sight.

"I wish to visit the Queen!" I shouted. "And I've come from so far away. . ."

"*Far away?* What is *that?* Heart to Heart has no distance."

"Well, the truth of the matter is," I hesitated, "the Rainbow Spirit brought me here."

"Why didn't you say *that* before?" answered the unseen voice.

Slowly the moss-covered steps between the gleaming towers came into view.

Gingerly I stepped onto them. My request had been granted.

Standing in this fabled land, seen through a veil of green, I beheld a wondrous sight.

The Kingdom was adorned in every imaginable shade and kind of green lushness—shrubs and vines, heather and pines, lawns and parks and orchards in lines, willows, palms, ferns and valleys, hedges and forests and fields. Surely this was eternal Spring!

But my joy was short-lived.

No one acknowledged my presence, nor welcomed me with heart; neither the gallant men in jewelled belts, nor the gracious ladies with pointed hats trailing in green chiffon, nor the maidens with emeralds woven through their flowing hair.

All I felt was rejection.

The Palace Guards, standing stiff as toy wooden soldiers dipped in cans of green paint, looked straight through me. Their heraldic swords, jewel-encrusted, moved objects by the mere wave of an arm. The courtliness and courtesy of people drifting by was impeccable. Everything about this enchanted land was familiar and untouchable. Like the fairy tales nurse often read, its bliss seemed unreal.

Yet no one paid attention to me.

Not knowing how to make my presence felt, I stood awkward in its midst.

A melodic hum, so enticing one could hear it forever, comforted me. Like chords of love, it wrapped itself around the Kingdom. It sprinkled the air with joy, inspiring devotion in all. Sounding within its song, wind-bells tinkled in the breeze.

I had to find them.

72

They belonged to a Minstrel Man, whose body swayed with the grace of a thousand green ferns. His crystal green eyes, deep as wells, awaited those who dared. Expansive as the waters of love, they beckoned the strong and weak. Sensing what might follow, I quivered.

For I hadn't expected directness with love.

"Eyes are the Heart of the Soul," he jingled his bells, staring straight at me. "Are they not open, even when closed?"

Pressing through the crowds, my shyness forgotten, I drew nearer. Stronger than my fear of refusal was my curiosity. Who was this strange man? What magnetism drew me forwards, to his soft and tender ways?

My body advanced, but my head stayed somewhere else.

And suddenly, amidst the love and happiness, a dark cloud came over me. A mood of confusion fell from nowhere.

"What are you doing?" screamed a voice. "He can only do you harm with his carefree, hearty ways."

"Where crowds gather, there is danger!" cried another dark voice. "Return to the corner you hide in, safe and warm it is *yours!*"

"Remember!" called a blacker voice. "Envy and jealousy protect you, sending everyone away!"

"Be generous! Better to see others happy than yourself!" cried another, causing me to doubt and waver on my path.

"Fight with the sword, not with the heart!" cried yet another.

My head swirled with confusion.

But the tinkle bells filled my ears, calling louder than these voices.

Their sounds moved my heart.

Gazing into my frightened eyes, the Minstrel Man just smiled.

His kindness tried to reach me.

For no reason and without a touch, I succumbed.

And my heart felt like fragile porcelain, about to crack.

"If your Heart is open, there is no pain," said Whisper.

The Minstrel Man laughed in his merry way, and began to play his bells.

> *Spontaneity comes from the Heart,*
> *Wonderment is where it starts . . .*
>
> *Memory resides in the Heart,*
> *Wanting to "see" is where it starts . . .*
>
> *Contentment with self comes from the Heart,*
> *Helping yourself is where it starts . . .*

"What will you give in order to receive? What will you extend in order to bend?" he smiled.

Could I surrender enough to follow the wishes of the Minstrel Man?

For surely he would lead me down the deepest ravine and up the steepest mountain—onto paths I never dreamed existed.

Watching me breathe anxiously, he just laughed and laughed.

I offered him my Cape of Protection.

"Let it become your Cape of Compassion," he said, returning it to me, "then with caring heart may you feel the joy and pain of others."

As he plinked his magical bells, together we danced on our toes. As we twirled through moss-covered streets, I began to feel the heat from my heart.

But our celebration came to a halt.

Marching directly towards us, in full green splendor, was the Queen's Royal Platoon.

My heart sank. I must have done something wrong again.

"We hope you find favor in Emerald City!" said the Captain with a courteous bow.

"Yes, yes, thank you," I nervously replied.

He gazed at me with as much curiosity as politeness permitted.

"We know not why, but your name has been called by the High Ones. We come to escort you to the Palace."

I sensed my stay was ending, although it had hardly begun.

Yet my heart opened wide, ready to receive what was coming next.

The Green Mirrored Gates silently parted, moving without a touch, obeying the wave of the Captain's sword.

A sense of mystery had returned.

Before me lay an incredible sight: an awesome maze of narrow paths winding towards the ivy-covered castle crowned with emerald towers. When we finally reached a sheltered garden, I breathed a sigh of relief. Its heart-shaped entrance and shaded bowers, thickly overhung with moss and delicately scented vines, were reassuring. I reached for a green-jade grape, but the Captain glanced in disapproval. He was already marching towards yet another arbored walk.

As the way unfolded, my sense of abandonment returned. Were these corridors never to end?

At last the Captain escorted me through a pillared portico, leading to a green fluorescent doorway. I stared open-mouthed at the sight before me. The Palace's Reception Room had walls quilted with shiny green satin, studded with dangling velvet ribbons, garlands, and green sequinned hearts. Its malachite floors were strewn with the finest tapestries. Green brocades covered chairs and cushions and couches.

My eyes danced from one thing to the next.

There was even a green marble podium, canopied with the palest of chiffons.

"What in the world is *that*?" I asked, for a moment unmindful of the grandeur of the surroundings.

" 'That' is where your audience will be held!" came the reply.

Then the Captain bowed and departed, as briskly as he had entered.

I watched him leave. And when I turned to the podium, it had completely changed.

Before me, enthroned, sat the King with his Queen of Hearts. In her crown sparkled a single, heart-shaped diamond larger than my hand.

Fortunately, I remembered to bow and curtsy.

And then it began.

"We have listened to your every thought, watched your willingness to change," said the Emerald Queen. "Indeed, you are a child of Light. Without judgment you have searched for truth. And in your trials you have listened to the words of others. Our Kingdom of Love greets you. May emerald rays fill your heart!"

"Watch carefully!" Whisper said, not wishing me to miss what was about to happen.

With a circular wave of her hand, the Queen sent a shimmering Green Ray into my heart. It occurred so quickly, I hardly noticed the luminous beam as it entered. Moments later powerful Green Rays still pulsed from my heart, spinning in coiled spirals.

As if nothing unusual had happened, the Queen inquired if I wished to speak.

Too stunned to ask about this unexpected gift, I chose instead to ask a question.

"Your Majesty, your Kingdom looks like the Earth, and yet not. What makes them so different? I cannot tell."

The Queen of Love continued to radiate green light.

"You see, child, hearts in your land are kept closed, like treasures guarded in a sealed container. Here hearts are expansive, filling both mind and body with Light. We radiate Love to everyone and everything. If one is receptive then Light shines around them. Darkness shields the heart from feelings. When hesitant to share, that which should be abundant becomes rare."

She smiled at me, her young visitor.

"The question you pose concerns the Heart of the matter. Life's secret is Love—the power that holds worlds together!"

She waved her arm. Now I saw what the Queen was describing—galaxies floating like diamond-dust in a sea of green.

"Every planet vibrates its own musical note. Together the notes make chords. These chords are but a small part of the unending symphony of the Universe."

I felt so complete, so open and at peace that I wanted to stay in this world of love forever and ever.

"What is 'forever'? Where is 'forever'? Does it hide in the crystal? Does it wait in the cave?" said Whisper.

How annoying to be jolted from reverie, back to some reality. So often, just as I was discovering peace, another piece of the puzzle appeared.

"What does Whisper mean by crystal?" I asked, aware that my thoughts were heard as clearly as if spoken.

"Radiant energy!" replied the Queen. "The Female, some say, is the cave's crystal. Rhythms of Love are her natural ways. Life's secrets are locked in her crystal."

"Yes, she's right!" said Whisper. "Crystal holds the Rainbow's Light. Light is Love, Love is Light. So *what* is the Quest, my dear?"

"If Light be everywhere, then Love threads the Universe," I murmured, not quite certain of what I had just said.

"Yes. Each Ray is but a facet of the crystal," added the Emerald Queen. "Together they glow with the Light of Love."

She beckoned me closer.

> *The Universe is infinite, crowded with stars,*
> *And many more planets than Venus and Mars.*
> *Each has its rhythms and seeds from its birth.*
> *They fluctuate, gravitate, fulfill their own worth.*
>
> *Had we left you on Earth, you would think "I'm alone,"*
> *And not understood that your home is not home.*
> *For 'home' is the stars and all worlds that combine.*
> *The Earth is just one among many you'll find.*
>
> *Your coming to us has helped clear your sight,*
> *We've shown you through Love all crystals unite.*
> *Our friend, the white Dove, will take you from here.*
> *You leave with our Love and our blessings, my dear.*

Green mist, scented with sage, lavender and rosemary filled the entire hall. Everything evaporated before my eyes. My dream was coming to an end.

Only myself and the white Dove remained.

I sighed, climbed onto his back, nestled into his silky feathers. I prepared myself to journey again.

The exhilaration of flying filled me with momentary joy. As we flew over the checkered green land, an oddity struck me. Far below was a small bluebird, lamely hobbling along, forlorn in this Kingdom of Green. So lonely and tired did he look that I wanted to give him comfort, ask how he lost his way.

Perhaps he, too, was leaving the Kingdom.

The white Dove, sensing my feelings, glided down towards the road.

And, just as swiftly he was gone, as if he had never been.

I felt myself stirring, awakening from a long, long dream.

Where was I?

The bed was not my own, the room was cozy but unfamiliar.

Not until I heard a tap on the door and the gray-haired lady appeared with honey, tea and biscuits, did I realize it was the thatched cottage. Had the forest grown dark? Had I stopped to rest here before returning home? Had I never left?

Perhaps it was something else.

"Am I bewitched?" I asked anxiously.

"No, no, my child," chuckled the old woman. "You have gone through a crack in the sky and although it feels like a dream, it is not."

"But I *did* leave here, did I not?"

"Only in a manner of speaking," came the evasive reply.

"Then what is going on?"

"You see, child, there are existences *between* dreams and waking. Silver Birds know of this twilight world. Some of us go there whenever we wish, others need to be guided. Dreams are often doorways to these realms."

This comforted me.

The old woman was the first person I had met who spoke of such matters.

81

Still I felt apprehensive, a bit overwhelmed.

"When we're ready, we slip into these spaces," continued the old lady, reassuringly. "After the shell has broken many Guardians appear, willing and eager to help one on the path. For then the egg of curiosity has hatched."

Again I felt lost for words.

But my first need was to be certain I had returned to the world of matter. My arm hurt when I pinched it, the old lady's hand felt warm. I had indeed returned to the physical.

"But won't everyone think I've gone mad?" I asked.

"Only if you speak to those threatened by the unknown," replied the old woman. "Blue lights dance around those who know these spaces. Does that not help?"

Yes, blue lights had blinked in the attic—that seemed so long ago.

"Explore the worlds you wish, but always return to your physical body. The guides will help you in this. You have chosen the Earth for this lifetime. Your attraction to *gravity* will be stronger than *light*. Here is where your commitment lies."

"Have you been *everywhere* and seen *everything?*" I asked.

The old woman smiled. "I have been to crystal stars that twinkle and heard silver bells that ring." And that was all she would say.

She tucked a warm blanket under my chin, kissed me lightly between my brows.

"Now, rest, my child. And remember—whenever you wish, you can always find the Bluebird of Happiness."

So it was that I fell into one of the deepest sleeps I ever had. Happily I drifted away, neither thoughts nor images in my mind, only feelings of Love.

VIII

The Sapphire Lake

*A*NOTHER ADVENTURE didn't happen for a while.
  And then it came unexpectedly. The day had been rainy and damp. I had snuggled into an overstuffed chair in the library, comforted by the blazing fire. There I read an adventure story: a tale of travels down the Amazon, a solitary voyage, a small raft pitted against wild rapids. It excited thoughts of hazards and boldness, challenges beyond bed and breakfast.

Thinking that way made me feel alive.

An adventuress in my dreamscape, I was willing to take chances. In my impulsive way, I did things my rational mind would never approve. Even though I hesitated and complained, the perils and risks excited me. Dedicated to wonderment and mystery, my craving for the "unseen" was insatiable.

The drama of the house held little interest. There I suffocated from overprotection, from rich food served on silver platters, maids in starched aprons and black uniforms, eyes watching what I was doing, curious and disapproving.

In the landscape of my dreams, there was no judgment—only lessons to be learned. Alone through choice, not avoidance, the issue was how far I could stretch myself. With these rambling

84

thoughts, I started to doze. Pages became moving words, then blurs. In trying to stay awake, I must have fallen asleep. Father removed the book from my lap, covered me with a mohair rug. I could hear him shuffling about, but no longer could speak.

As I went deeper into sleep my "inner movie screen," projecting the film of my mind, appeared. The first image I saw was my friend, the bluebird, no longer hobbling and sad, but rather cheering me to come.

Without hesitation, I followed.

No sooner had I done so, than I felt foolish. Doubt was my worst enemy. Why had I wanted to see him? There was no good reason. A blankness fell across my mind. The bluebird disappeared into blackness—the blackness that always followed blankness.

Now what should I do?

By carefully reconstructing the details of our first meeting, a small grey shadow crept in. Then a kind thought brought the bluebird back again. Sensing my uncertainty, he tried to help by entertaining me. He plumped up his feathers, strutted about, brilliantly imitating the song of a nightingale.

Yet I remained unmoved. Only when his feathers expanded into fan shapes did I allow myself a little smile.

"Come, ride with me," he suggested, unsure if I was ready to leave.

"Oh, why not?" I replied. Having jumped on so many birds' backs, there was nothing to it. My companion's wings spread and flattened like a magic carpet.

But he never spoke again.

I frowned. Had my mind gone blank again? Was *he* larger and me the same, or *me* smaller and he the same? Had I again lost my sense of scale, as well as my grasp of time and space?

"Whisper, Whisper," I called. "I need your help!"

"Come now, Aisling," my friend replied, "open yourself to chance and see what happens. Stop hesitating before you start."

No sooner had I taken a deep breath and relaxed, than a great gust of wind hurled us into space. I felt us rise from the earthly plane. We soared through the sky, sailed invisible oceans of air, began loping, diving, piercing cushions of clouds. My eyes smarted as we crashed through blinding vortices of wind.

The bluebird remained steady and undaunted.

I desperately held onto my Cape of Compassion which was wildly flapping like a second pair of wings. So fierce was the storm before us, my very essence seemed threatened. This could not be an ordinary reality. It must be a test of endurance. The tempers of spirals, windfalls, rotating currents of whirling air challenged us, as if we had undertaken to combat Nature herself.

I hoped my Guardian of the Air knew where we were going. But the way he guided in silence demanded my trust, and I was determined to get through this obstacle, to meet it with steadfastness. Nothing was going to stop our adventure. Giddy with courage, exhilarated by the tempest, I smiled a secret smile. As long as I kept my faith, things seemed simple.

When the storm cleared, a curious sight was before me.

Below us lay a glistening lake, dark as sapphire. Its mirrorlike surface reflected indigo mountains and soft meadows of blue flowers. In the distance rushed a gushing waterfall of the clearest azure blue. Its spraying mist veiled yet another mountain.

Could this be a painting on glass?

As we flew closer, I tried counting the different types of flowers —lavender, periwinkles, morning glories, forget-me-nots, delphiniums, cornflowers, gentians—and others I had never come across before.

"Can you see the plum trees and blueberry bushes hugging the lake?" I shouted.

But the bluebird's mind was somewhere else.

In a few moments it became clearer that what had seemed to be a lake was not. Instead of water, below us lay a huge sapphire that in every way resembled a lake. And the waterfalls, instead of gushing, were petrified ice frozen in air!

"Have you ever seen anything like that?" I gasped.

But my pilot paid no attention. He was concentrating on finding the gem's exact center, the spot where he must leave me. It was as if *he* were following instructions.

"*Who* is talking to *you*?" I finally asked.

He did not answer.

Skillfully he touched the glassy surface. I climbed down beside him. Without a word, my companion, like the dove before him, fluttered his wings in the briefest salute, then flew away.

"What am I doing *here*?" I said to myself.

I visualized myself looking foolishly around, sliding across the lake shouting for help, and at last reaching the safety of the shore. Then I thought to sing my troubles away, like Edward did at home. Finally I imagined myself being rescued by my distraught parents, who had just awoken to the fact I was missing.

These images made me serious again.

Just by thinking, I could turn what looked like a dream into a nightmare.

Except now the beauty and strange stillness of the landscape began to absorb me. I sat down cross-legged and listened.

The sapphire's peculiar qualities caused me to be silent within. Its deep blue light encouraged thoughts of contemplation. I remembered the times when, alone in the forest, I had felt the

serenity of the tall trees with their dark shadows. And what they had given me was not unlike the sensation of calmness just before sleeping.

Yes, that was how I felt now.

But this mood was not to last.

As soon as the thought told me how I was feeling, the sensation was over.

A strange ringing sound was beginning to fill my head, especially in my right ear. I had heard it many times before. Often, a faint buzzing meant that Whisper was calling, but I could sense he was not around. Anyway, this pitch was unusually high and shrill.

Just as I thought it might hurt, it turned into bells and chimes, then full orchestra. The tones were magnetic, drawing me towards them. They were soft and melodic, yet other-worldly. I had never heard music like this before.

"What on earth is going on?" I wondered.

The music abruptly stopped.

"Oh, may I hear it again?" I asked whoever or whatever was creating it.

But nothing happened.

Thinking the sounds had come from below, I peered into the sapphire's polished surface. To my pleasure I saw lovely blue angels with transparent wings and twinkling toes swimming within the gem. They appeared and disappeared with the swiftest of movements.

"Are you the bells and chimes?" I asked politely.

They responded with such delicate musical clatter that I knew I was right.

But what of the full orchestra?

Perhaps that had come from above.

I concentrated again and, as the music welled up in all its glory, I imagined myself within it. It seemed to lift me from the ground, carry me away. Never had I heard so many instruments, been surrounded by so many chords. I must be in the center of the universe, with all its magnificence around me, above and below, sideways and upside-down. No matter which way I turned and twisted, the volume stayed constant and strong. It entered every pore of my body, changed my sense of balance.

Just as I was feeling ecstatic, becoming one with the music, it ceased.

Then the lake stilled, no sound was heard.

The silence was so intense it unnerved me.

"Whisper, Whisper, are you there?" I asked.

No answer came.

Once more I surrendered to the unknown. By sheer effort of will, I remained still. And as my trust deepened, so did the sapphire's color. Soon it was the same indigo as the surrounding mountains. Now it became difficult to see shapes, for a dark blue haze fell on everything. And I was drifting towards it.

It carried me to the waterfalls, onto the crystal ice.

This was the *last* place I wanted to be. A moment ago the world had expanded around me, an oasis of tranquillity, filling me with new possibilities. The depths of the sea and height of the sky had seemed reachable. Now I seemed trapped.

All that greeted me were cries and pleas.

> *We are* thoughts *frozen in time and space,*
> *Useless energy that has no grace.*
> *Do something, Aisling, so we might flow,*
> *And you shall see all crystals grow!*

I focused upon the iced surface. Being absorbed into its essence, I felt what it was feeling. A curious message followed. Trapped by the blue Demon of the East, its flow had been held in course. Perhaps a magic potion, some chosen words of power, an offering needed to be made.

"Tempt the devil, try his hand, and you will be in zombie land!" a horrific voice shrieked at me.

"Touch the water, turn its face, and you will join another race!" shrilled yet another voice.

Threats did not bother me.

Becoming one with the wall of ice, I entered its hardness, felt its rigidity. The pain of its torment reached my heart. I struggled to visualize it as melting, thawing, turbulent, moving into sparkling, refreshing, clear and free water. Giving me the sensation of flying, the water swept through me as it gushed and flowed, whirlpooled, rippled and waved.

"Let the *thoughts* flow downriver," said the Spirit of the Waterfall. "Let them come and go, rise then fall, moving with the stream."

"Flow like the water and, at the same time, be still as the mountain," it continued.

Not attaching to these thoughts, letting them come and then float away, I concentrated, without grasping, and stayed serene.

"Thoughts out of control swirl in the whirlpool of words," came the next murmur.

"Be solid as trees and rocks and mountains, but stay free as the running water!" it sounded again.

Each thought dissolved, carrying me with it.

Soon my head was clear of internal chatter.

I became a floating leaf following the stream of life. Neither

whirlpools nor eddies stopped me. The flowing water guided me. Gushing sounds, whirls and vortices, whooshes and turbulence became calm, rhythmic movements as the stream spilled into the sapphire lake.

First I was a pebble in the flow, then a rock in the stream, next a boulder grown into a mountain.

I looked up towards its very peak. My gaze reached its summit. And who should be there, waiting for my ascent? The very Spirit of Blue, delighted by my accomplishments!

"Welcome to the mountain of mystery, the passageway to Light!" she exclaimed. And, as she smiled at me, the dazzling blue light around her intensified.

The brilliance of the light should have blinded me, yet its fierce embrace brought no harm. I wanted to tell the Blue Spirit about my recent adventures, but decided not to.

This realm was still too new for me to speak about it intelligently.

"Within the *dark*, you'll find the Light," chuckled a familiar voice.

But I was too intent on the Blue Ray to start solving riddles. I made a mental note later to ask Whisper where he had been.

"The treasure of this mountain is more precious than any jewel," said the Blue Spirit. She looked benevolently at me and opened her hands in invitation.

"Our Kingdom of Blue is the spiritual part of your Quest," she went on. "You have seen how through faith and trust and detachment you opened to new experiences and changes of vibration. Surrender and devotion are the beginning of soul awakening. No evil spirits can reach it—they can only place obstacles in your path."

Here you'll find calmness and quiet and grace
With which to help others who are seeking their place.
Now enter the mountain and there find the cave,
You'll see in the darkness, you'll meet what you crave!

The Blue Spirit pointed towards a narrow path that wound its way through the dense shrubbery clinging to the mountain.

And so, with a shy wave, I set off on another stage of my journey.

Before going forward, I looked back.

But the Blue Spirit was gone.

"Oh well," I thought, "as soon as one friend vanishes, another one appears."

Suddenly, in sheer relief, I laughed aloud.

The sound echoed and re-echoed around the mountain, as if all the Guardians were sharing my pleasures and making light of any fears I may have had.

I waited until the last echo died away, then began to walk the twisting path and, before I knew it, I found myself standing at the entrance of a cave half-hidden by overgrown vines.

There was nothing to do but go forward.

And this I did, with a strange mixture of courage and caution.

IX

Shadows of the Cave

No SOONER HAD I EXPLORED the mountain's side, than a small, dark door, hidden by overgrown bushes, attracted my attention. And when I entered within, this concealed entrance closed behind me.

There I stood—trapped in a musty-smelling cave with no apparent light source. Yet it was clear enough for shadows, and I could dimly see where I was.

"Anyone at home?" I called, certain even as I did so that nothing and no one would answer.

The old, uneasy feeling was with me again.

I began to have horrors of insects coming out of the walls, unexpected little animals scurrying across the earth floor—ants, scorpions, rats, beetles, snakes. At home, in my protected room, nature never entered through the bedroom door. Only in my dreams. Feeling vulnerable and creepy, I investigated with my eyes.

Finally, driven by curiosity, I began exploring the cave, but found it uninviting. Its walls crumbled at the touch of my fingers, its dankness penetrated my skin. Even the acrid smell of the chamber cut through me. Ghosts and phantoms seemed to float through the air. Nervously I brushed them away with my hands. Only the stillness reassured me.

"What am I doing here?" I wondered. Surely there was a better place to be. Finding a rock to rest against, I considered my predicament.

I closed my eyes as if to sleep, and immediately felt a throbbing between my brows. My forehead was pounding as noticeably as my heart. Placing my fingers between my eyes, I tried to find out why. Nothing changed until I released the pressure. Then pulsations started.

Pictures formed in my head.

First, a blackboard with writings and numbers on it. Then a screen showing films, flickering with fragmentary shapes and images. They sped by so quickly I could barely keep up with the changing pictures. Next colors streamed past—extraordinary colors I couldn't identify.

Now I was watching planets and stars, tunnels and spirals and stairways, spaceships and rockets. Each time I tried to hold the image still, it escaped. Whatever I did, the picture stayed only a moment. I could neither control nor direct it. And when I tried looking closer, it vanished altogether.

"Things happen when you stop trying," whispered a familiar voice.

I remembered to relax and breathe deeply.

Behind my closed eyes, the screen flashed indigo. Little golden spirals whirled by, expanding each time they crossed the screen. The brightest one trapped me within it. I started spinning, drawn as if into a whirlpool, rotating with ever-quickening speed.

As I moved within its orbit, my body became weightless. The golden glow became a spinning tunnel drawing me deeper and

deeper into the indigo screen. The closer we came to the light, the less I was aware of my physical density.

Yet somehow "me-the-observer" remained detached, wondering what was going on. Too many Aislings seemed to be floating about.

"Have you ever watched yourself moving through your own dreams?" asked Whisper.

"Yes, of course," I replied, feeling my life *was* a dream within a dream within a dream. "But am I dreaming *now*?"

"No, no, you are just beginning to break the shell of the dimensions. The crack has not yet appeared. Nor has the energy switched."

"Then what shall I do?"

"Stay with the whirling spiral, become *one* with it. Let yourself go!"

I obeyed these instructions and immediately my confidence returned.

Round and round I swirled in the golden spiral as it gradually narrowed towards its base. And the moment I reached its still center, the change occurred—the direction of the spiral reversed. As the motion turned anti-clockwise, I was spun into another time and space.

Where did it take me?

To the Silver Bird waiting before an open garden gate!

Following my old friend, I found myself entering a dark, mysterious paradise overgrown by trees of violet blue, so laden with fruit and foliage that their branches swept the grass. Oversized flowers blossomed everywhere. Birds chirped songs that moved through the still air in waves of vibrant colors. There was so much to see and smell and feel that I didn't know where to turn.

A weathered bench invited me to sit down. It was sheltered by willow, oak, jasmine and plum, all shimmering in the amethyst twilight. Looking about, I suddenly felt dwarfed by the lushness of my surroundings. The Silver Bird took on gigantic proportions. He had the strangest luminous light around him. He seemed to send me energy to speak.

"Will anyone come and talk to me?" I asked.

In an instant, a monumental, shadowy form appeared. As it drifted towards me, I could just make out an ancient figure who, like my other guides into these inner worlds, was transparent and faintly luminous. I could look *at* him and *through* him simultaneously. I stared, for his fluffy white beard almost reached his feet.

"Hello! Who are you?" I asked.

The Old Man remained so still and thoughtful, I immediately regretted having spoken first. This was the first barrier in all my travels that truly felt impassable.

Looking at me with the patience of the ages, the Old Man leaned on his crooked staff.

"I, child, am the Gateway through Space and Time. Do you not recognize me? Do you not know who I am?"

I hesitated.

Several preposterous ideas crowded into my mind. Was he Father Time or Saturn? Santa Claus? The Man in the Moon? Perhaps he was the Old Man of the Universe? Only one thing was sure—he was a familiar figure, perhaps even a friend. But without a name. Many, many times he had appeared in my dreams, astride a crescent moon, beckoning me. Sometimes he would be standing on a mountain's peak, waiting for me to come towards him. Hesitant and shy, I never did either. He was too awesome.

I even saw him in legends and fairy tales nurse read to me. But,

in the dreams, he came alive. He always watched me silently, from a safe distance, waiting for me to seek him.

Yet he had never stood so close before.

The directness with which he had posed the question undid my confidence. I shrunk further inside myself, now to the size of a pea.

This only amused the Old Man.

"Why should I let you pass?" he said, looking down at me. "I am the Guardian of your Universe, the Keeper of Time, the Doorway to Space, the Gateway through the Sun into the Galaxy. I guard the realms where the signs of the Zodiac have replaced the hands of the Clock."

I bristled.

Whenever challenged, my stubbornness reasserted itself, with a vengeance. Imposing and authoritative he might be, but I was *not* going to let him stop me from going where I was supposed to go! Mustering all my determination, I visualized myself as majestic and as tall as the Old Man himself and, with crystal clear vision, looked him eye-to-eye.

"You are indeed a spirited child," he chuckled, "to challenge such a one as I! Come then, I shall take you to the lands known to the Silver Bird. But remember—speech may be the Bridge of Time, but silence is the Bridge of Space."

With that, the Old Man took my hand.

The joy and anticipation I felt at this moment easily surpassed anything I had experienced on the Quest so far.

X

The Mind Tunnel

THE NEXT STAGE OF MY ADVENTURE BEGAN. I continued to hold the Old Man's hand, feeling secure in his authority. He seemed a curious combination of the Old Woman's wisdom and Whisper's magic.

"Close your eyes, child, and tell me what you see," he directed.

Again, I found myself looking at my indigo screen.

"There's a long tunnel in front of me—very, very dark—with faint light at the far end."

"Very well, then that is how we shall travel. Imagine yourself within it, and we shall begin."

No sooner had we entered this tunnel than we started to drift along, carried by a gentle wind. Although nothing could be seen or felt, the silence that encompassed us was somehow comforting. I was surprised not to be bothered that my feet were not touching the ground. Floating around the tunnel's curves, following its dark and empty course, I found myself being drawn closer to an understanding of its mystery.

"Is this a time tunnel like the White Rabbit and his funny hole?" I inquired, pleased with my comparison.

But the Old Man's head did not turn. It was as if he had neither heard, nor wished to hear, the question.

I sensed myself out-of-time again. I still wanted to connect all the people, places and things I had seen. I needed to put them in a framework that was solid and secure.

How could I find the thread to sew them together? All I seemed to receive were fleeting images, tantalizing glimpses of new places and new experiences.

I dearly wanted to stay long enough somewhere to feel at home there.

Yet a link was still missing—one that was beyond Whisper and the Silver Bird and the Magic Garden.

The Old Man had no intention of helping me while I was looking backward.

On and on we went. Nearer and nearer came the light at the end of the tunnel. It was so dazzling, so electric, I thought for certain to be burned to bits. But coming closer, the flickers, instead of piercing, passed me by. For a moment I had forgotten I was a light body travelling through the time tunnel.

Brilliant streaks were bombarding me now, yet I was shocked to feel nothing. I still couldn't adjust to the sensation of things going straight *through* me.

Only seconds before I had been standing with the Old Man. Now I had lost his hand.

Where had he gone?

Was I expected to continue alone?

"Trust, trust, that you must!" said Whisper, tired of saying it again.

I simply ignored him. The heat was flowing, the light throbbing, the colors singing.

And suddenly, as my light body energized, I found myself by a gentle waterfall overhung with flowering vines. In the middle of a clear pool at the foot of the fall sat a frog on a rock.

"Riddick! Riddick!" croaked the frog, as if to remind me how ridiculously easy it was to do everything here. Just think yourself somewhere, and—presto!—you were there.

"Bathe in water, bathe in light, bathe in everything that's bright!" babbled the frog.

Some way off, staff in hand, stood the Old Man, watching me.

I took courage to ask him if water was light, as Whisper had once intimated.

"Everything is light," came the Old Man's reply, "but water is the light of purification." He indicated the pool. "Refresh yourself, my child, the journey ahead requires a new kind of strength. Yet all is within your reach."

So I bathed, listening to the chirping of the birds, the tumbling cascades, the frog's rhythmic croaking. It was an all-too-brief moment of Paradise. But in a world of change, nothing stays still.

"Come, Aisling, the celestial bells are calling."

Without questioning I joined him, cleansed and refreshed. The Old Man indicated our destination—a distant seven-tiered mountain whose peak was veiled in soft blue light.

We set off, floating effortlessly through a sky as clear and pale as aquamarine. As we approached, the mountain seemed to be enormous, forbidding. I was tempted to ask, "Why are we going *there*?" But I remained silent. Learning to still my thoughts and hold my tongue had been a long and arduous task.

Perched on the mountain's peak and veiled in the filmiest cloud was a tiny chapel or abbey. Silent monks were walking around in hooded, dark brown robes.

We landed before a blazing fire, one whose radiance illuminated the chapel's grounds but somehow threw no shadows. It was unlike any light I had ever seen. Everything I looked at seemed to be lit from within.

In the presence of this powerful, uncompromising energy, I experienced a serenity I would never have believed possible.

"It is the flame of the Spirit that dwells within all," said the Old Man reverently.

A small monk approached and bowed, indicating that we should enter the chapel.

It was only then that I noticed that he, and his fellow monks, had neither hands nor face.

The Old Man touched his fingers to his lips and I understood.

Inside, the chapel positively glowed with warmth. Subtle music was coming from somewhere, but there was no orchestra to be seen.

"Remember the symphony of the stars?" said the Old Man. "Well, here it never ceases."

Hearing the music, watching the silent monks, I was filled with happiness. As my guide and I moved forward, the monks moved aside to create a path for us. Multicolored light streamed from a stained glass window, falling on us like rainbow dust.

It was the colors that were creating the music.

I began to feel dizzy, ecstatic.

Everything was dissolving into light.

The monks faded in and out of my vision, their robes turned ash white, their cowls became stiff and pointed. They appeared and disappeared in rapid succession.

Was it the music, the rainbow light, the burning candles, incense, the altitude—or what? I could easily have wept for joy. I had never felt such emotion before.

The Old Man understood my predicament. "The atmosphere at this level is intoxicating," he said. "You must remain detached or it will overpower you."

"But I'm overwhelmed," I said softly.

"That is just as it should be. You are meeting the Brotherhood, the silent teachers of your plane. They have come to witness your passage into the next dimension."

"Have I ever met them before?"

"They attend you always. Some have been your personal guides, extending courage when your faith was ebbing, sending hope at times of exhaustion, awakening your sixth sense, the threshold of the unseen."

"Why have they neither hands nor face?"

"Because their need for personal identity is long passed. These beings no longer seek personal acclaim. After many lifetimes on Earth they learned to rise above negative suffering and doubt. They sought the positive vibrations of light and compassion. And when they completed these teachings a choice was offered them. Did they wish to experience other galaxies, or to return to Earth as teachers? The members of the Brotherhood chose to serve as invisible guides to your world."

"But, if they're invisible, how am I seeing them?"

"One light being sees another. The Indigo Ray opens the Third Eye, that which can see what was invisible before—what you call 'seeing' in dreams. Aisling, have you not arrived at the place you have waited for?"

"Yes," I hesitated. "But why do they come and go?"

"To test your ability to move through different currents of energy. Being masters of the energies, the Brothers can appear and disappear at will. As you are discovering, the further you explore, the more sensitive are the vibrations you require."

"Is that what is happening to me?"

"Protected by a guide—yes. For you are not yet ready to be alone. There are galaxies with electrical energy so intense that you would burst into flame the instant you entered them. To travel in one's spirit body, you must adjust. Never forget, there are many, many more energies than you imagine." He smiled encouragingly. "There is always something more to discover. Seeking never ends."

The Old Man of the Universe stepped aside.

A curtain veiled the chapel.

Solemnly encircling me, the Brotherhood formed seven rings of vibrant colors. I recognized all of the colors except the violet, which I had not yet encountered. As the circles turned, faster and faster, so the music whirled and intensified. Soon only colors could be seen, and then only white light, a brilliant vortex of energy carrying me higher than ever before.

I felt myself rising as if in a cyclone, then entering a library with stacks of glistening books, silent guides and a long wooden table for reading.

Abruptly my eyes opened. I was still nestled in the soft chair, surrounded by my father's books, the fireplace was glowing, the room warm. I shook my head, wondering what that was all about.

"Some libraries are for reading, others open doors to what we need," said Whisper.

Instinctively, I felt he was right.

But, still, before exploring further, I would wait for the Old Man to return, to take me to night school again.

Why did a sadness overwhelm me? Awakening in the family library, having no one to speak with, made my loneliness acute.

My old desires loomed strongly. If only I could share these experiences, receive someone's advice, surprise, even shock. At least receive a reaction.

Perhaps nurse would listen. I might say:

"Sometimes I hear lingering music, and see Spirits with wings and hooded faces. Have you ever heard of such a thing?"

And nurse would answer, kindly but firmly:

"Of course, my dear. All children do. Not to worry, you'll soon outgrow it."

"But they're *real*," I might add.

"Only in your dreams, child. And we know that dreams are make-believe."

Then I would stop myself from telling about the Old Woman and Whisper and the Rainbow Spirit and all the other things that really mattered. I could pretend everything was fine, just as most grown-ups did.

In this moment of discouragement, Whisper was helpful:

"Apples fall from trees when they're ripe. Learn the sounds of the wind, the tongue will come later."

And so I remained silent, hoping everything would turn out all right.

XI

The Crystal Hall
of Records

DURING THE EARLY MORNING OF SLEEP, I found myself in the darkened mind tunnel searching for the Old Man of the Universe. He was waiting after the tunnel's first curve, pointing to the light which shone steadily in the distance. And when its brightness increased, I sensed a new part of the journey was beginning.

I let myself travel forward with my companion into the dazzling light. I found myself caught within thousands of golden sparkles. As their energy ran through me, making my whole body tingle, I felt myself becoming one with their magical brilliance.

But that rare, timeless moment, sometimes called "forever," ended abruptly. The Old Man pointed to a tiny opening within the dancing light, indicating that we were about to travel through it.

When we reached this barrier, another peculiar thing happened. I felt the Old Man's eyes in the *back* of my head. I was seeing *through* them, as if they were mine. I now knew where we were going without being told.

And so it came as little surprise when we spiralled downward and landed in an underground valley. Nothing amazed me anymore.

Here I felt the presence of many invisible beings, phantoms

115

from another time-frame. Perhaps they had chosen to come here between lifetimes, for they felt more human than spirit. They were too intense in their projects to notice us. Or perhaps the Old Man was a frequent visitor to these parts. I wondered whom else he might bring here.

"We are below the Earth," explained the Old Man. "Remember what you see. We have come to find a special cavern."

We drifted past shadowy caves and dark passages, beings illuminated by a greenish-blue light, and finally glided through a large opening into a cavern, empty but for long oval mirrors and a suspended crystal ball.

I stared at the crystal. It floated in space, held by nothing whatsoever, and lit the entire chamber with soft golden light. I craned my neck to examine it more closely. I wasn't certain if it was swaying or my own eyes were moving.

The Old Man was so quiet that I had almost forgotten his presence.

All the while he was watching me being magnetically drawn into the crystal. I was seeing pictures come and go within it. The one that fascinated me was of a monumental, marble building surrounded by classical columns.

"Would you like to go there?" asked the Old Man.

No sooner had I agreed, than I found myself inside the marble colonnade surrounded by staggering columns. I looked up at a strange shaft of light descending through the sky, and realized that it converged in a V-shape where I was standing.

Before I had time to wonder, a scribe appeared.

"Bathe for a moment in this white light," he instructed, "then we shall proceed to the Halls of Learning. Its books are always waiting for those who travel through crystal, entering the fourth dimension."

I did as bidden, then followed him along several dark corridors, passing reception halls and lecture rooms, all of them filled with transparent beings in long robes. There was no sound anywhere.

We came at last to a huge library overflowing with documents, scrolls, shelf after shelf of books, and visitors studying quietly.

"We are in the Universal Library, the Hall of Records," explained the scribe, in waves of thought. "Here, every lifetime you have spent on Earth is catalogued. Each existence contains lessons, as you now know. Those you successfully mastered have been translated into energies elsewhere. Here you will find records of lives left incomplete, either in experiences to be undergone or knowledge to be acquired or debts to others repaid."

He gave me a reassuring smile, then continued. "Some of the characters in your own particular drama you meet in lifetime after lifetime. Others you encounter only once. It is to discover these things that you have come here."

This information was beyond my wildest imaginings. I found a chair at one of the long wooden tables and sat down, hoping to acquaint myself with these new surroundings.

"What a busy place this is," I thought, watching scribes bustling about and visitors intently reading. They went through volumes of books in seconds, as if breathing rather than reading them.

Shyly I examined the many marble shelves and their uncountable rows of books. Then something attracted me. One volume in particular was glowing with golden light.

"It's *yours*. Take a look!" murmured Whisper.

Suppressing my excitement, I took the enormous book from its shelf and laid it gently on the table before me. I lifted the brown leather cover, expecting to see pictures and beautifully penned words on parchment pages.

But what confronted me was a hollow—an opening.

"Look into it," prompted the scribe, who still remained at my side. "See what energies and images form. Find what teachings await you. This is a living book, a Book of Life. Worlds are there that you have forgotten exist."

"Now what do you see?" he asked after a short pause.

My eyes widened. "Why, there's a crystal shining in the darkness."

"Then return to it and receive its message."

To my astonishment, one moment I was staring into the book's hollow, and the next I was *inside* it. Instinctively, I launched myself into the surrounding vastness, spiralled into another existence. And almost at once, far below me, faintly visible, lay the pyramids of ancient Egypt, majestic in their timelessness and solitude.

I could almost taste the hot dust and feel the rising heat stick to my skin. The grandest pyramid shone like a polished gem in its setting of dull gold.

Now its walls became translucent, revealing what lay beneath—a second, inverted pyramid beneath the sand, converting the monument into a glistening diamond octahedron. Images began to float in and out of this double pyramid, making a decision necessary.

Should I investigate the passages above ground, or seek the subterranean levels? Should I fly around the outside? Or go inside to explore?

My indecision lasted only a moment. Then my thoughts took me below ground, down and down steep steps that led—somehow I knew this already—to a point aligned with the upper pyramid's apex. The odor of damp earth was everywhere. There was no light, but I sensed where we were going. Everything was familiar. Was this not the secret part of the pyramid where the priests gathered for their ceremonies? Did they not receive their instructions here, from voices not seen? I could remember shafts of brilliant light at these times.

"My, my, how splendid you look in your priestess black robe!" whispered a voice I had half been expecting.

"How did you know where to find me?" I asked rather ungraciously.

Whisper was amused. "Ah, that would be telling, wouldn't it?"

"Well, this is one trip I'd like to do on my own."

"Thus do buds blossom into flowers," he replied cheerily, without any attempt to explain his brief reappearance. And, for the moment, no more was heard from him.

But Whisper had been right again. I was indeed wearing a dark priestess robe with jewelled collar. On my feet were golden sandals, my hair was thick black and straight and severely cut. My eyes were painted with black kohl. A crown with snake and scarab symbols encircled my head. Bracelets adorned my arms and anklets.

"Who *am* I?" I wondered.

Deeper and deeper I descended, drawn by some unknown energy towards a chamber in the very heart of the pyramid. In this mysterious room was a magnificent crystal sphere with gold coils in it—exactly like the crystal in the cave of the Old Man.

Now, priests were studying it intensely.

"What are you looking for?"

They seemed astonished by the question.

"We are awaiting your presence, High Priestess, so that the transmission may begin."

I hesitated. For an instant I was neither myself *nor* the female in the ordained robe. Certainly I didn't know which body I belonged in.

"Center quickly, my child," encouraged the Old Man of the Universe, concerned lest my vibrations fall lower than the chamber's, for then all would be lost. "Look deep into the crystal, concentrate, it will bring you back to where you are!"

As I watched, a huge eye formed within the crystal, its iris shimmering with blue fire. It grew steadily until the entire crystal flooded with the same golden light.

Then I remembered.

As High Priestess I had studied this very crystal, understood its receiving powers, learned to transmit its energies, knew the secrets of its light. I remembered how its vibrations healed our bodies and we, in turn, had healed others. Ages past, these priests had been my friends, my helpers, my supporters in times of trial and unrest and discovery. One even had the eyes of my father of today.

But they had always sought *my* guidance, not me theirs.

Unsure that I wanted to see more, I froze. My memory faded. I had completely forgotten what to do next, where to go, what, if anything we had accomplished.

"Return to the mountain cave," commanded the Old Man.

I did so instantly, and was relieved to be back with him again.

"What is happening to me?" I asked.

The Old Man smiled.

"You have slipped between time frames into an old memory pattern. When past, present and future merge into the now, such an event can happen. Then you may revisit scenes from many places in the past, or enter the future." He beamed with pleasure. "Your Egyptian lifetime was a splendid one indeed. But beware, there were others of much less attraction."

"What made me so frightened?"

"Because they called on you to perform, and the energy was too strong for the Aisling of today. It overwhelmed you. Instead of joining that existence, you remained detached. By not centering you lost both confidence and concentration. Even so, you saw much that can be drawn upon whenever needed."

"What made me return to Egypt?"

"Its memory was strongest for you. Each lifetime has its lessons. Sometimes we revisit previous lives to remind us of things we mastered then, or failed to master. Or perhaps to forgive ourselves for things done badly, people we offended. A glimpse of the *then* can help us cope with the *now*."

"But I didn't stay long enough to see. And there was so much about crystal to learn."

"Shall I remind you that you already know its properties? Your momentary lack of trust only prevented you from refreshing this memory. To receive from any time frame, we must be clear as crystal itself. No matter, it is all experience. Are you willing to try again?"

I hesitated.

Was I ready for these explorations, or had I overreached myself? The more I travelled, the less I understood where it was leading. Suddenly, surprising even myself, I turned on the Old Man, the one whom I trusted and depended on.

"What is *real* in all this?" I demanded to know. "Nothing is what I think it is. Am I just trapped in one long, recurring dream? *And who are you exactly?*"

This time the Old Man understood my frustration and did not sympathize with it.

"I am whatever and whomever you want me to be. And I can create whichever place or plane you wish to visit. We are all crystals dissolved into light. Anything we wish to be, we are!"

125

"Well, who am I then?" I asked struggling to keep up with all this. "And what am I to *you?*"

The Old Man replied with a smile I did not understand.

"What is before you is all there is," he said. "You cannot call one thing real and another illusion, for they are the same thing. Each contains the other. Only the Now exists—past, present, future are all compressed into the One. That is the only possible answer to your question. Your existence is the one you experience the moment the question is asked. Only by reconciling reality and illusion can you become the One."

I nodded. "Then whatever happens, I should accept and understand for what it *is* and not keep questioning it."

"Exactly! To understand that there are more realities than one, and more illusions than one, is to begin to know the multiple Universes."

I needed time to digest this apparently simple information. I smiled a shy, diffident smile. No longer could I dream of asking the Old Man what or who he was.

"Perhaps I should add just one thing," he said, "and this is deceptive. Reality is what you *cannot* see, and illusion is that which you *can.* And yet illusion is born in reality and dissolves back into it. Everything in your galaxy is undergoing constant change. Illusion is that change. And so *you* live in a world of illusion. Your spirit or essence is real, nothing else. It is this that remains the same throughout, never changing in all your lifetimes."

I frowned. "How does crystal relate to all this? I am still not quite clear."

The Old Man gestured and, as he did so, pictures of crystals, tunnels, planets orbiting in space flew through my mind. I had everything to do to concentrate on what he was saying.

126

"Crystal is the barrier which keeps you on planet Earth," he explained, "the passageway to the next dimension, the fourth. The mind tunnel takes you through Time, the spiral carries you through Space. Crystal is frozen light, neutralizing and cleansing your energy fields. It prepares you for travels to places beyond. All ancient cultures have known this."

I could handle no more thoughts and had no need of further questions. I was ready to move on and find out for myself.

"Fix your gaze on the crystal," said the Old Man, reading my mind. "Visualize yourself within it."

I took a deep breath, quieted myself, then merged effortlessly with the crystal's electric energy. Immediately I was surrounded by brilliant dancing lights, then, unexpectedly, by cell after hexagonal cell, exactly like a bees' honeycomb, endlessly repeating each other.

I stepped through one section, only to face its replica. Then another and another, unfolding as I advanced. Faster and faster I travelled through the honeycomb.

But a distant voice checked me in midflight.

The Old Man wanted me back.

The faintness of his voice told me how far into the crystal's structure I had ventured. Reluctantly, I envisaged the cave of learning and, in a flash, returned to it.

"Why did you call me, just as everything was turning into a kaleidoscope of color and light?" I asked.

"Take care, child," cautioned the Old Man of the Universe. "Crystal is a transformer. Your physical self waits while your *mind* enters the crystal and takes on a light body for travel. Only in this way are you able to meet light beings from other realms." He wanted to emphasize the need of protection. "You must know

how to reverse the process so as to return to your body. As you are not yet experienced enough to do this alone, a guide watches over you."

I nodded, but wanted to know more. "What makes crystal so mysterious, so magical? Why is it on fairies' wands? And wizards and gypsies and fortune tellers—why do they look into it?"

The Old Man was careful to choose words as simple as the subject itself. How often did men bury simplicity under complicated scientific theories, superstitions and wild imaginings.

"All through the ages," he began, "wise men have known that crystal is a most powerful memory bank. It vibrates with electric pulses. In it every thought is imprinted, recorded and stored. Of all the substances on Earth, it is most like living matter."

"So that's why it took me to the Hall of Records!" I said.

"Precisely. Crystal is the only material on Earth which holds this knowledge. To enter it is to know."

"What are the gold coils in this one?" I indicated the glittering sphere suspended above us. "And the one in Egypt?"

"Coils of electrical energy. As Priestess, you knew how to channel the sun's energy in your crystal and send it throughout your working chambers," explained the Old Man, deciding to stretch my mind. "Combine the sun's energy with powerful thoughts and anything can be created. For those who are trained and disciplined, there is nothing that cannot be called into being or removed from the physical plane."

The information awed me, even if it *was* something I had known about in a previous life. All this knowledge seemed beyond my immediate grasp. As doubt crept forward, the Old Man slowly faded from sight.

But I was not left alone.

"Receive first, experience later," whispered my trusted friend.

"Oh, Whisper, am I ready for these teachings?" I sighed, remembering the Silver Bird and bluebird. We had travelled in silence and now that seemed comforting.

"Looking back is not the way of learning." he said. "That which presents itself, you are ready to receive. It is your next step forward."

"Do I bring to me whatever happens?"

"Precisely so," agreed my friend, "your invisible vibrations call everything into being. You are your own magnet."

I needed time to rest, and to take in the wisdom that the Old Man and Whisper had just imparted.

Yet I was not to rest for long.

XII

The Kingdom Under the Sea

AS I ENTERED MY NEXT DREAM VOYAGE, the Old Man of the Universe stood within the waiting crystal and, beckoning me to follow, began to disappear into its depths. Anxious not to be left behind, I obeyed.

This time I felt myself racing downward into the greenish sea. The legend of the King of the Ocean flashed through my mind. This realm was said to be ruled by a great fish who wore a crown and guarded a sacred pearl in his stomach. The only way to obtain the pearl was to swim through his mouth, down to his belly, and fetch it.

It was a tale nurse told me often.

Even as these thoughts passed by, a number of fishes of all sizes appeared, tempting me. I entered the mouth of the grandest one which opened into a series of doors, each space growing progressively lighter.

The final door—or was it a giant pair of jaws?—led into a huge suite of bone ivory rooms. The middle room was circular, with bizarre transparent tubing running from floor to ceiling. Its walls were sectioned into many squares, forty nine I counted, all flashing in random patterns, none of which I understood. I had

131

been spinning, travelling at great speed, yet in this room I felt solid. It was the silence, the lack of vibrations that made me feel secure. Even the flickering lights made no sound.

Eyes seemed to be watching me from the flashing lights, from all sides, waiting to see what I would do next. The room closed in on me, then expanded, leaving me unsure if it was moving, or I was moving.

Ignoring the shifting light patterns, I forced myself to concentrate on the transparent tubing in the center of the room. As I did so, it began to spin, pulling me backward, forward, sideways and, finally like a vacuum cleaner, towards it.

Before I could do anything to resist, I was *inside* it.

It felt as if the Spirits had taken me over.

For I was in a huge mushroom, being pushed towards the cap at incredible speed. Around me fluorescent colors became word patterns. The words slowed me down, the spaces between them became wider.

I was engulfed in water again. Had I returned to where I began?

And *where* was the Old Man? I desperately needed to speak with him again. But he was nowhere around.

I was not alone, however.

His place had been taken by a huge fish decked with metallic scales and rainbow fins that turned on hidden hinges. I heard the Old Man's words, ''I am whatever and whomever you wish me to be!'' Had he, indeed, transformed into this magical fish?

Now I was speeding forward. Not only was the creature rainbow-colored, but its colors changed with every movement, rippling the undersea around us.

The great fish veered away, and I held onto him, our path determined by shifting light patterns that seemed to come from

133

within the fish. It steered away from sharks and octopusses simply by changing colors and sending out spirals of gaseous bubbles.

"I will show you some secrets of the sea," said the fish. Instead of hearing spoken words, I received his thoughts telepathically— in my mind!

"How lovely," I replied in the same way, "but I can't see a thing."

"Use your sense of hearing, not your eyes," he advised. "Here we move through sound, our bodies are antennae in motion. Our every movement is carried through water as a wave pattern. We *hear* objects more than *see* them."

"If you lived among us," the fish continued, "you would rest your eyes. When something is near, my *mind's inner eye* tells me its size and intentions. My feelings tell me if it's moving towards me, and whether its purpose is to pass or attach."

"What if it wants to destroy you?"

"Then I agitate the waters around me, sending fierce currents of shock waves towards it, veering it away. Or I move aside, and let it pass. How can I be harmed?"

Allowing no more questions, the metallic-scaled fish rushed me through a succession of strange tunnels and tubes. The last one was deep indigo blue, exceedingly narrow and with little light. I condensed myself by thought, travelling with ease. I wondered if I, too, had turned into a fish.

We emerged facing three underwater cities, blue, yellow and green, contained in crystal domes, all interconnected by tubular passages. A shaft of piercing white light shone upward from the center of each city.

I looked quickly for a guide. Immediately a manlike creature with very long fingers, green scaley skin and pointed ears appeared, wearing a silver diving suit. Wordlessly, he directed me towards another tunnel leading to the first city.

Standing in its crystal blue dome was like being enveloped by a cloudless summer sky. The entire space was transparent blue with tall, angular buildings and squared balconies, not unlike those in cities in my own world until I went within!

For inside each building, all rooms were circular and the atmosphere was charged with secrets, alive with hushed vibrations and a sense of guarded projects being carried out.

Now my guide was pointing at a large circular door.

"Go through," he instructed, "but take care to close the door behind you. It must be left secure!"

I did so, and found myself in a deep blue chamber like soft velvet. I was immediately aware of greenish beings studying me. Trapped and uncomfortable, wondering what was going on, I "heard" a silent voice.

"This chamber is an energy accumulator, transmitter, receiving rays and beaming them into the Universe. These rays vary in frequency and purpose: vibrations, numbers, sounds, colors and thoughts. Now, steady yourself, and ride the yellow beam, the Ray of Clarity."

The Watchers instructed me to lie on a white marble slab, pointed my fingers towards a polished, faceted diamond set in the ceiling. My back began to tingle. I felt myself enter an inner sanctuary, heard faint voices discussing the connections between this realm and the three-dimensional world.

I wondered if I was going home.

Was I "inside" other worlds? I had once read about places within the Earth.

Fearlessly I rode the Yellow Ray. A burst of light from the diamond sent me speeding through blinding golden shapes, shimmering rainbows. At last I arrived into what seemed to be the Yellow City.

I was in a room where scribes busied themselves writing mysterious signs and shapes, drawing circles upon spirals. One of the scribes, staring into a crystal, was receiving information about a cone-shaped diagram he was making, divided into seven sections, each corresponding to a color vibration. The cone was a three-dimensional spiral, violet at its apex. As the tones spiralled downward, opening into a gentle S-curve, the colors delicately merged into white light.

"This will be a huge structure," a voice told me, "built in our city when we rise from the sea to create new lands. This cone will transport us to your world of three dimensions. It then will be a place you will not recognize."

"And when will that be?" I asked, astounded.

"In the year with the number eight," came the reply.

The scribe looked out the window, pointing to a series of little spiral discs being shot out of the neighboring domes.

"Those are messengers, scouts for the underwater cities," he explained. "They are the dolphins, and very helpful they are to our people."

"What are they doing?" I asked, remembering that dolphins were thought to be exceedingly intelligent, although few knew exactly how or why.

"Gathering information. They report events on Earth and underwater simultaneously. They're called the computers of the sea, for they have a memory bank far exceeding your wildest imaginings."

Now the sea-man pointed to a flight of steps, indicating that it was time for me to leave. As soon as my foot touched the first step, it turned into a shattering shaft of green light.

Instantly I found myself in the domed Green City.

It was a computer city, a huge raised platform with banks of computers everywhere. Green beings wearing laboratory coats and metallic belts showed me machines for processing data. Inserted into this apparatus were special tapes with bars at either end, one constant, one variable. The variable bars consisted of various solid materials whose grooves matched specific patterns of rays sent from green bars. I was astounded—the machine transmitted messages from other light beams!

"We have added equipment that operates with heat and sound waves," I was told.

"How does it work?"

"We mentally imprint writings onto tape, and when rays are projected through the tape onto a flat white surface, the resulting light patterns contain the message."

"How far can information be sent this way?"

"We can reach distant planets because our transmitters rotate, emitting wave lengths in any direction we choose. Come, I will show you."

I was led to a hexagonal tower, onto whose summit descended a beam of intense white light. Inside the tower, a bank of generators was drawing power from this strong light. I thought of the Egyptian pyramid, which once had used the sun's light as dynamic energy.

"Enough power is produced for the entire city. And from this we accumulate rays for later thought transmissions." The guide took my arm. "But come—you must see our library."

139

He escorted me to a circular room which reminded me of the Hall of Records. The library was lined with volumes—thousands and thousands of books—yet the center table was noticeably bare.

On it rested a single volume bound in soft brown leather, inscribed in Old Gothic type. It was an ancient and important-looking book.

"What is that?" I asked.

"Records of a land you are soon to visit," he replied.

I remembered no more, for I was floating effortlessly away from this green underwater kingdom towards wakefulness.

I opened my eyes, then immediately half-shut them again, shielding them with my hand.

The sun was shining on the trees outside my bedroom window, gilding the upper surface of their leaves.

Yes, I had returned home.

Watching the play of sunshine and shadows, I lay drowsing for a while. I wondered if there was a connection between the sun's rays and the mysterious light rising from the towers in the underwater cities. Since visiting the Hall of Records, my curiosity had become strange indeed. The ease of fantasy had been replaced by wonder. I couldn't imagine what might happen next, or where I might be guided, or what I might even learn.

But what intrigued me most of all was that extraordinary book.

Where *was* it taking me next?

XIII

The City of Golden Gates

SOON I FOUND that just thinking in bed was not enough. I needed someone to respond to my questions. My mind craved answers.

I wondered what had become of Whisper.

"Are you dreaming dreams again?" he instantly asked.

"No—more like wishing wishes," I replied, slowly pulling my bedcovers closer. "I'm wishing I could travel backward in time or into the future—alone."

Somehow the darkness of night brought about these longings.

"Just try, then. Think of your first visit to Earth, when you flew through the skies with your black cape spread to the winds. . ."

"No."

"Or those years huddled by the fire—wrapped in tattered shawls and skirts for warmth, an ancient seer forecasting things to come. . ."

"No!"

"Or your lifetime without speech—the child-mute in white robes, speaking in signs, sharing thoughts in silence. . ."

"No, no!"

"Then the one in which you begged, near starvation, trying to escape the slipping mud?..."

"No, no, no!"

"Then *which* past or future do you want?"

"The one from the soft leather book under the sea!"

"Atlantis?"

My eyes widened. "Atlantis! Yes, I want to know where it is, what it means, how to get there!"

"Then you must do what you already know. Close those restless eyes, call upon your inner visions, let yourself fall backwards in time and space."

I was already revolving in my mind, spinning out from the top of my head, in reverse spirals, somersaulting to the Atlantean time-frame, to the City of Golden Gates.

I landed upon sheets of ice, then slid down a bleak tube into subterranean levels, passing frozen mammals with grass still stuck in their teeth.

Then the tunnel's cold chill turned to warm air, and I reached the "city that once was."

Before me was a glory that was staggering. I was nearly blinded by the golden temples, gemstones imbedded in marble columns, roads lined with precious metals, walls covered with silver and copper and gold. Never before had I witnessed such wealth, such opulence.

But this pleasure was short-lived.

Something was quaking and crumbling in the atmosphere itself.

I was given but a moment to scan the precious shrines, the lapis lazuli palaces, the intricate network of golden bridges. Then I

144

was whisked away towards the marble stepped pyramid, into Poseidon's temple, through the Golden Sphinx's corridors.

The scene I came upon was solemn, joyless.

Priests, wearing azure blue robes, huddled fearfully together as the High Priest of the Sun spoke the words they had so long dreaded to hear.

I strained to understand what was being said. Phrases about laboratories mating humans with animals, "centaurs" of a new race, reached my ears. I heard arguments about test tubes and apparatuses used to lengthen human life, then murmurs about turning hot and cold springs into gold.

I needed someone to explain all this.

But first the pronouncement came.

The gods were angry. Their wrath was soon to be felt. The giants of Atlantis had become a nation of careless priests and black magicians. Had not the gods come to Earth, mingled with these very men, and once taught them the Sun's wisdom? Had not their knowledge been abused, their energies misdirected?

The elders shook their heads in disbelief.

The verdict was too harsh, they said. Atlantis could not be destined a third time for destruction. Would this not mean another ten thousand years in oblivion?

As the discussions began, I watched the radiance of the sun begin to fade.

The priests knew only too well that the sky rippled with electric currents, the air itself radiated heat waves, and that power without wires was theirs. They could call on the atmosphere for everything they needed.

They knew the code of the crystal.

They had trained others to amplify electricity by storing energy in special crystals. They had shown that crystals could generate more energy than they received. And this was not all—they had also taught others to harness the Sun's rays through crystals and store the energy in power stations built under the earth—to concentrate light waves into fine laser beams for building and reaching long-distance goals.

I tapped the shoulder of one priest, trying to get his attention. He turned towards me, tears in his eyes, unable to utter a word.

For the accusations continued.

Because of the arrogance, wantonness, decadence, depravity, of the people of Atlantis, the day would soon turn into the darkness of night.

The priests wondered. Had they been wrong to reveal their mysteries to those who quested for power? *Who* among the people they had instructed had abused this knowledge on such a scale that everything now had to be sacrificed?

Through the misuse of solar energy their beloved Atlantis was to fall.

Again, I looked towards the priest next to me. I didn't understand why they had not stopped their people from amassing weapons of destruction, made by the laser energies of the crystal. Why were there even stockpiles of solar destruction awaiting release? Had their opulence made them decadent? Is this how they had lost their power?

Obviously the gods had returned to pass judgment.

Atlantis would shake from volcanic upheavals, tidal waves, earthquakes. Fire would clash with water. Gigantic rainclouds would open. All would be covered in a sea of mud.

The priests closed their eyes in horror.

Once again I tried to make contact, to speak, but a council meeting was being convened. I moved with the others and found a

146

place. The tension was mounting by the minute, as the elders considered the terrible judgment.

"We must prepare to scatter to the corners of the Earth—to Yucatan and the Americas, to the Pyrenees and Morocco, to Egypt and the Bahamas. Our records must be given to the Sphinx of Egypt, our crystal to the Andes, our sacred relics to the Mayas. They must be sealed in time capsules, to be opened only when man is again ready for cosmic knowledge."

As objections rang out, I gasped. Would this also happen to the Earth I knew? Was it not filled with abuse and destruction, chaos and men hungry for power? Suddenly, the scene before me merged with my "real" life and became something more than a view of the past.

The priests were arguing that it was not wise to leave so little evidence of their glory, their cherished wisdom.

And so it was agreed that duplicate relics should be left in sacred places of highest vibration, in the hope that some, at least, would survive.

I watched the tension of that hour drain the color from the priests' faces. I witnessed their telepathic powers in action. All I could do was remain silent.

Images of spacecraft appeared everywhere.

They were calling up their ships—cylindrical craft that sailed through air and water alike, their engines guided by crystal gyroscopes. It was these very ships that had first brought the Atlanteans to these islands, and took them to other dimensions, following the magnetic lines that permeate the entire Universe. Now the ships would follow the Earth's own radiations and take the guardians of the secret wisdom to safe lands.

The time was drawing near.

Darkness was encroaching.

"Our sacred treasures must be hidden in caves where water cannot reach them. Walls must be inscribed with symbols that can be read. We must preserve our science of sonics, our beloved crystals, our methods of transferring beings from one dimension to another. . ."

But it was too late! The cataclysm was already upon them!

A comet, a great flaming snake, soared from the moon's silver disc, hurling its red anger at the City of the Golden Gates.

I was flung into the sky, witnessed the land already in the throes of tidal waves, disappear within moments.

And so Poseidon sank beneath the churning water, buried again beneath the ocean for another cycle of ten thousand years.

I found myself, once again, hovering over the Egyptian pyramids. It was peaceful here. There was no anger or recrimination, no destruction, no war between darkness and light.

Time had shifted. Perhaps it was many hundred years later.

Thinking myself there, I entered the Great Pyramid. Two priests, now black-robed and solemn, awaited me. Together we followed a deep shaft leading directly to the pyramid's apex, into a room smelling distinctly of burning metal, but metals unknown to me.

It was a museum of vehicles used by previous peoples for space travel.

Spherical objects, looking like diving chambers with wires coming out of them, were being inspected by other priests. To our Egyptian eyes, these Atlantean craft were positively antique. We were puzzled by their construction. In adjoining rooms priests were experimenting with solar energy, hoping to discover how these relics operated.

"Perhaps we should search in the Andes," I heard one priest mutter.

Vaguely, I remembered about a crystal hidden in those mountains.

But then the scene abruptly faded.

Suddenly I was travelling beneath the Earth's surface in a strange flying machine. Somewhere, somehow, spaceships had been hidden in these parts.

Were there space travel stations underwater?

Were they part of lost Atlantis?

The number seven kept flashing in my mind.

Of course, I remembered! Seven entrances led down into the Earth. One of them had taken me to the forgotten land of Poseidon beneath the sea, some others would lead to the Earth's womb, to the ancient people in caves.

Already I could *feel* but not *see* them. I *knew* but could not hear, *sensed* but could not touch.

The flying machine was diving through the underground route into yet another space-time frame. I realized an ancient memory was returning me to something I already knew.

But what took place was more than I anticipated.

XIV

The Moon Boat

WHEN THE SPACECRAFT ENTERED the subterranean tunnel, my only impression was of a kingdom with greenish light and faint whistling noises.

The pathways before me spread like fingers, fanning in every direction. Here was a subcontinent, a network beneath the Earth, a staggering system of passages, flowing streams, caves, empty niches, wells and spacious halls. It was a giant labyrinth, a citadel, a monument to some cataclysm or, indeed, another world. Lime-green fluorescence illuminated this domain, causing plants to grow to great heights, preserving carved objects in their original state. Everything had a sense of the supernatural.

I felt immersed in long-forgotten history, amidst tombs of another time, amongst phantoms waiting to share their tales.

The sanctuary's walls hid secrets. Surfaces were covered by lines suggesting words. Drawings depicted ancient lore. Stones radiated a violet light. And from all these symbols came sounds.

My head buzzed with excitement, my fingers reached out.

"Seek the code, not the word. Speak to the amulet, not the stone," hinted an old, familiar voice.

I had completely forgotten about Whisper. Once again I wondered how he had found me.

Then everything started to tremble. As I lost my balance, almost fell to the floor, the walls mysteriously lit with sacred objects. Faint writings moved on the oblong stones. Everything quivered, including my body. I was not certain whether to touch anything or try to stay still.

As so often before, a guide appeared.

This time the majestic figure was severe in his silence, direct in his actions. His piercing look and flamboyant presence did little to relax me. I stepped backwards. He reached for his sword, pointed to symbols illuminating the walls. First, a Sacred Eye, then a metallic Sun disc, next a quarter Moon, shaped like a boat, flickered before my eyes.

"There are men in the Sun, held by sounds," he said. "In silence such tones are heard, evoking both Sun and Moon. *Listen* and you shall learn the Journey of the Soul through its spiral of life."

What kind of a realm had I entered now?

I turned my eyes towards the left, only to discover yet another exotic being. Immaculate in white, his hair strangely blown, he half-smiled as he pointed his Moonboat in my direction. Hardly had I expected the wall's symbol to be at my feet! In this vessel of Light the three of us explored the underground maze. But there was little progress, for we circled around and around.

"Spirals and circles engraved in walls, circles and spirals move through halls!" teased Whisper.

I did not pay him any heed, for I had recognized these patterns from prior travels: the spiral held everything together, the moving force of life. Its clockwise turn had kept me earthbound, its reverse spin had whirled me into other space-time frames.

But what of the circle?

"Don't I go through the Sacred Eye at the beginning of the mind tunnel, and meet the Sun disc at the end?" The words slipped from my mouth.

The magnificent one smiled, gestured full circle with his sword, and materialized a copper shield! Rays of light beamed onto it, then bounced back like rods of energy. It looked like the Eye of Fire, with reddish gold and mauve tones. Was it a polished disc to catch the Sun's motions? Was this perfect circle a priest's magic mirror? Or simply a circle of Oneness?

Carefully I looked into it.

"I'm seeing a sunburst, a circle with lines radiating from it. Someone is walking along one line, someone else along a second. And inside, a circle is being drawn within the circle, and another within that. Oh, I'm in a spiral again!"

"Concentrate on the rays, not the center." prompted Whisper.

I had forgotten the thin rods coming from the disc's circumference.

"Look, they're shining like metal." I exclaimed. "They're antennae, rays picking up sound currents, changing from silver to copper to gold. I'm hearing one thing and seeing another. I heard 'solar' and saw waves of motion."

Without being told, I merged into these images, hoping once again to hear the heavenly music. Instead, there were currents of sound, electric movements I did not yet understand.

"Only in the center is there silence," said Whisper.

I remained puzzled.

The Moonboat was gliding past burial chambers. Hidden behind rows of mummified bodies lay silver relics, gold figurines, copper vessels, sacred statues. Frozen in a state of drifting hibernation, they seemed out of time. I felt, somehow, I could reach them through sound, unlock the secrets guarded so long.

155

Below, resting on a pile of ashes, shone a magnetic black onyx ring.

" 'Tis a ring of Saturn—the gem of bewildering dreams," explained the noble one.

How often the combination of mystery and beauty tempted me!

Carefully, I slipped the ring onto my middle finger. Instantly I was before a Temple of the Sun, one tucked in a gloomy valley caught between indigo mountains and blood-red craters. A priest, facing sunrise with arms pleading, was praying to his gods for help.

Moss-covered and cracked by dryness, the once majestic seven-stepped pyramid now lay decayed, surrounded by crumbling courts and weed-filled terraces. The underground passageways still lay in onion-shaped formation, a cross section of tunnels clearly reminiscent of the Moonboat journey.

"Onions are circles of the Universe, bringing tears to one's eyes so that one may 'see' better! said Whisper. "Their rings mark the planes into which creation is divided!"

This was beyond me. All I wanted to know was where I was.

"About to witness another misuse of energy—the spiritual downfall of the Aztecs!" came his reply.

Priests, in ceremonial pointed hats, were bowing to the High Priest, splendid in his headdress of exotic bird feathers. I gasped at the beauty of his cape, richly beaded and feathered, depicting clouds and blue sky, rainbows and waterfalls—a cloak of the four elements. Obviously he commanded the energies of earth, air, fire, water. But his finery held the power. Without it, I sensed he was a frightened and desperate man.

"There is a legend," Whisper said, "of gods appearing to men, flying in celestial capes."

"Surely these priests aren't pretending to be gods?"

158

"Perhaps trying to call them to Earth again?"

But now I was following the procession of priests, wondering if I once had been among them.

Moving silently along dark, damp corridors, we arrived at the one remaining sacred chamber. Here the opulence was staggering. Relics of silver and gold, diamond and sapphire, jade and turquoise were everywhere, culminating in a sun-shaped disc twice human height, bursting with golden rods. Like the one in the tunnel, it was of solid copper radiating an electric energy of amber and violet.

Despite my fascination, I experienced only discomfort.

"What smells so peculiar?" I asked a solemn priest nearby.

"We burn a strong incense, infusing all visitors with an invisible wax, sealing their thoughts, ensuring that temple secrets will never be revealed. Certain death awaits any disobedience."

The spell being cast made me more than anxious.

I felt evil energies were being invoked for purposes of black magic. My intuition told me to leave quickly, before caught in its spell. In my hurry to exit, I found myself trapped in an inner court-yard—witness to a ceremony that was unbearable.

Within a circle painted in blood, lay piles of minerals and crys-tals, enormous gems and translucent stones, heated by blazing torches. Around them danced marked and feathered men, whirl-ing checkerboard shields of copper and onyx. Watching them was hypnotic. For a moment, I felt myself being drawn into the sorcerer's web.

Then I saw priests removing these sizzling objects with long, silver tongs, placing them on the skins of screaming victims. Others were using obsidian knives to tear out the still living hearts of sacrificial humans. Everywhere blood spurted and tor-tuous sounds shattered the air.

159

Desperately, I called to the Old Man of the Universe to rescue me from this ghastly scene.

Reliable as always, he immediately appeared.

Silently taking my shaking hand, and wrapping me within his cloak, we flew far above the Aztec pyramid, towards the most majestic mountain.

"*What* was that about?" I weakly asked, still trembling from the horrors just witnessed.

"Atlantean secrets, hidden in underground tunnels, were discovered by the Aztecs, then perverted for black magic," he explained. "They, too, misused their knowledge. Destruction by solar energy was but a small part of the story. Thinking to please their gods, wishing more power and control, priests in both civilizations practiced sacrificial rites. They believed the gods would return in their favor, bestowing the powers now lost. But such misuse turned on them, for evil done to others comes back upon oneself with equal force. So it was that both empires perished by the very means of destruction they had once created."

I listened in silence. The message was clear: as we treat others, so others treat us.

The Old Man continued to explain.

"You see, young one, upon your Earth are pockets of energy, powerful receiving and transmitting stations. All vibrations remain dormant until aroused. Then they are used for good or evil purposes. Therein lies humanity's choice. In a world of dualities, energy shifts in either direction. All action brings about reaction. Only stillness creates peace."

"Free will is whether you listen to your inner *or* outer voice," interjected Whisper, the philosopher.

"And who, pray tell, are *you!*" I finally asked.

"Whomever *you* project me to be!" came the reply.

The Old Man pointed to an alignment of constellations above our heads.

But I was still thinking about the Aztec pyramid, wondering if a crystal was buried beneath it. I felt its rays to be alive and powerful.

"Come, Aisling," encouraged the Old Man, intentionally intruding on my thoughts. "Another civilization must choose how to use that sacred stone. Now I shall show you how to ride its rays in the opposite direction."

"You mean travel *into* the stars?"

"Exactly so," replied my guide.

The stars seemed so close that surely going to meet them would do no harm. I wondered what the Old Man would tell me. Night school seemed to have an unending curriculum.

Smiling with assurance, I confidently committed myself to the next journey—ready for whatever the stars might unfold.

XV

Beyond the Rainbow

*I*T WAS NOT WHAT I HAD EXPECTED.
For in the distance, an exquisite rainbow, pulsating with every color in the spectrum, was arched across the sky. I watched it change into a double-rainbow, enticing me to come.

"Rainbows are the bridge between worlds," Whisper said before I flew towards it.

I pictured myself encompassing all the colors, filling my heart with their lightness, then floating across the rainbow bridge. Yet, I found myself not on a bridge at all, but inside a gigantic multi-colored bubble. It was a throbbing diamond, an explosion of prisms, forming hexagons of many colors; dazzling blues, greens, ambers, yellows, oranges, violets, crimsons, corals. I was happily caught in a wonderland of dazzlement.

"The colors are trailing into the sky!" I shouted back to the Old Man. "They're in spiral formation, like a comet, carrying me into space. Oh, I'm becoming a slender spiral!"

At that point the Old Man joined me. Taking my hand, he lifted the sky's curtain and led me through.

"You're entering another realm," he cheered. "Follow its impulses. Your soul-body will take you anywhere you wish."

164

Spinning counter-clockwise, I gasped as I saw angels with silver-white wings, planets with sparkling rings spinning around them, spaceships moving along fine golden lines. A green planet with a violet-coral aura caught my attention. "No," I thought, "I'll go there another time."

I felt myself moving into "something" that was "everywhere" —on all sides of me.

Positively astonished, I shouted, "I'm in a whirlpool of sounds, buzzing and rotating around me, like millions of fireflies in the air."

"Become One with the sound, then wait for the form," Whisper encouraged.

Now I was amidst glistening stars and luminous shooting objects whizzing past me at incredible speeds. Pointing to one star, the Old Man reached out, lovingly touched it as it sped by.

"Are you *certain* they're stars?" he said with an enigmatic smile.

Delighted to show me this inner universe, he began peeling the darkness away, unveiling worlds within worlds—and still more worlds. Cautiously peering into a star, I saw a little world, light years away, with miniscule planets going around inside it.

"Stars *are* planetary systems," he said. "Now are you sure that stars are stars?"

But I wasn't listening.

I had discovered one world looking exactly like the Earth, only grey and black. It seemed to be a negative image of my home planet. I flew closer, intrigued, believing I saw a child playing in the woods. Then I realized the child was myself. I turned to the Old Man for an explanation.

"Your present life was imprinted there," he said.

I watched this child call out, heard her cry echo and re-echo. But no one heard—just like those times at home, calling into the darkness for someone to come. Then I saw the child grow smaller, going backwards in age, a baby, then tucked in the womb, then flying in the sky trying to choose which mother to enter. Never before had I realized that *I* selected my parents.

"Perhaps you were one of the stars before that," laughed the Old Man.

He looked at me with a twinkle in his eye, then continued.

"Your mind knows everything, and every existence you have ever experienced. It waits patiently for you to unfold your own unconscious."

"Is that who Whisper is, my intuition? Is that why he knows so many things before I do?"

"Yes!" said my friend. "Whisper belongs to your supraconscious, that part of you which recalls all time-frames and what happened in them."

"That's why everything he says is so familiar, like something I heard long ago."

"Exactly!" he smiled. "But this sensitivity becomes a distant memory at your time of birth. The cells of the physical body contain unresolved emotions from previous existences. Usually the conscious mind is unaware of this. The supraconscious, your eternal memory bank, is clouded by mist as each lifetime begins. When awareness comes, the fog slowly lifts, and Rays of wisdom show themselves."

"And when your sleeping soul awakens," chirped Whisper. "then you and I journey through the land of far memory."

For a change, I was speechless.

The Old Man waved his staff of the ages. Together we watched

167

the gray black planet transform into the Moon. Before us lay its dark side, a mass of dead, spinning rock.

"The Moon and the Earth, your unconscious and conscious, were once in balance," explained the Old Man. "Moon beings were not unlike Earth people. That is when the atmosphere was the same, before the split occurred. Something is coming to verify this past relationship, but not quite yet. Suffice it to say that many Moon myths will come true."

"But when did the Earth and Moon stop relating?"

"After a gigantic explosion from the Moon's center, reacting from the Earth's insecurity and imbalance. Red dust, coming from the atmosphere, spread everywhere. That happened three times. First in long ago cataclysms, then the last time helping to destroy Atlantis."

"Was there ever harmony between Earth and Moon bodies?"

"Yes, yes, my child," answered the Old Man, "but that was in the beginning of all beginnings. First came balance and excitement, then indifference and discord, then a breaking apart. From continuous internal strife came bloodshed and war, the Moon and Earth each defending their position. But relationships never end, they simply change. The Moon still affects the Earth, in tidal waves and myths. And the Earth reminds the Moon to stay awake. Like all opposites, they are inseparable."

"And what is happening *now?*"

"The Earth's center is cracking, as the Moon's once did, for pressures are mounting, and man will soon explode. He has created so many 'things' that he cannot find his inner core. Changes are rapidly coming. As the Earth loses its center of gravity, no longer attracting the Moon, then will disaster occur."

The Old Man pointed to the silent stars, indicating their patterns would change as well.

"Many disturbances will occur," he said, "and major constellations will explode. Then man will realize he looks through a darkened lens hardly seeing anything at all. Only transformation will move him around the spiral."

I suddenly felt what it could be like—the Sun and Moon, existing in harmony. Between them was a central core, spiralling outwards in a coiled vortex of dynamic energy.

"Yes! Yes!" the Old man confirmed. "Spirals are the balance between the swinging pendulum! As each turns in the spiral, so another harmony is reached. Before experiencing a new awareness, one experiences the spinning outwards, the whirling around and around, the confusion before the calmness of the tranquil *center.*"

"Then the Quest is a returning to the still, quiet point!"

"Yes!" said my guide. "And stillness will turn to movement again."

"But the spiral will only turn after the still point has been reached!" I gasped.

Were all my travels just to learn this one simple truth?

The Old Man of the Universe drew me into movement again, this time directing my attention towards the Milky Way. Its carpet of glistening stars was almost more than I could stand. For that's how I had felt in the center's stillness.

"There is a navigational map of the sky," prompted the Old Man, "known to those who experience these states. It is an intricate mesh of golden lines. Forms, whether objects or light bodies, move along them, thrust forwards by the spiral. Using this vortex energy, at velocities faster than light, they pull themselves from one dimension to the next."

"From one spiral to the next," I added with pleasure.

"Spaceships first spin in a vortex of bright orange and sapphire blue. When they join the golden light, they are on course."

I wondered why the Old Man was saying this.

He looked at me, smiling with the sadness of a friend now departing. He called up a vision of the double Rainbow, and the Magic Mountain, to remind me of the roads I had travelled.

But surprisingly my interest was somewhere else. A light brighter than the surrounding stars had caught my attention. Its movement did not harmonize with the pattern of the sky.

It was a silver spaceship, hovering beyond the seven-tiered mountain.

"Now I must leave you, young one," said the Old Man of the Universe, "and return to the Garden of Twilight. My guidance ends at the edge of Moon. Remember the Silver Bird, the one who appeared in golden light? He will guide you to the spaceship. Now, continue your Quest, for it never ends."

Without waiting for my reaction, the Old Man disappeared behind the Mountain and Rainbow Bridge, leaving behind him an echo of love and encouragement.

I hesitated.

Was I ready to go on another journey? Where would this silver spaceship take me? Should I instead return home, snuggle by the fire in my father's library? Was my mother waiting to kiss me good night? Had nurse finally noticed my disappearance? Was Edward singing without me?

And what of the dear Old Lady who lived in the woods?

The Silver Bird turned his head towards me, indicating a beam of violet light calling us to the spaceship.

Summoning all my courage, I climbed onto his back.

As I gazed into the star-filled universe, a familiar voice came to me.

"Trusting is not knowing where you are going! And faith is the path of heart!"

Then no more would Whisper say.